CONTENTS

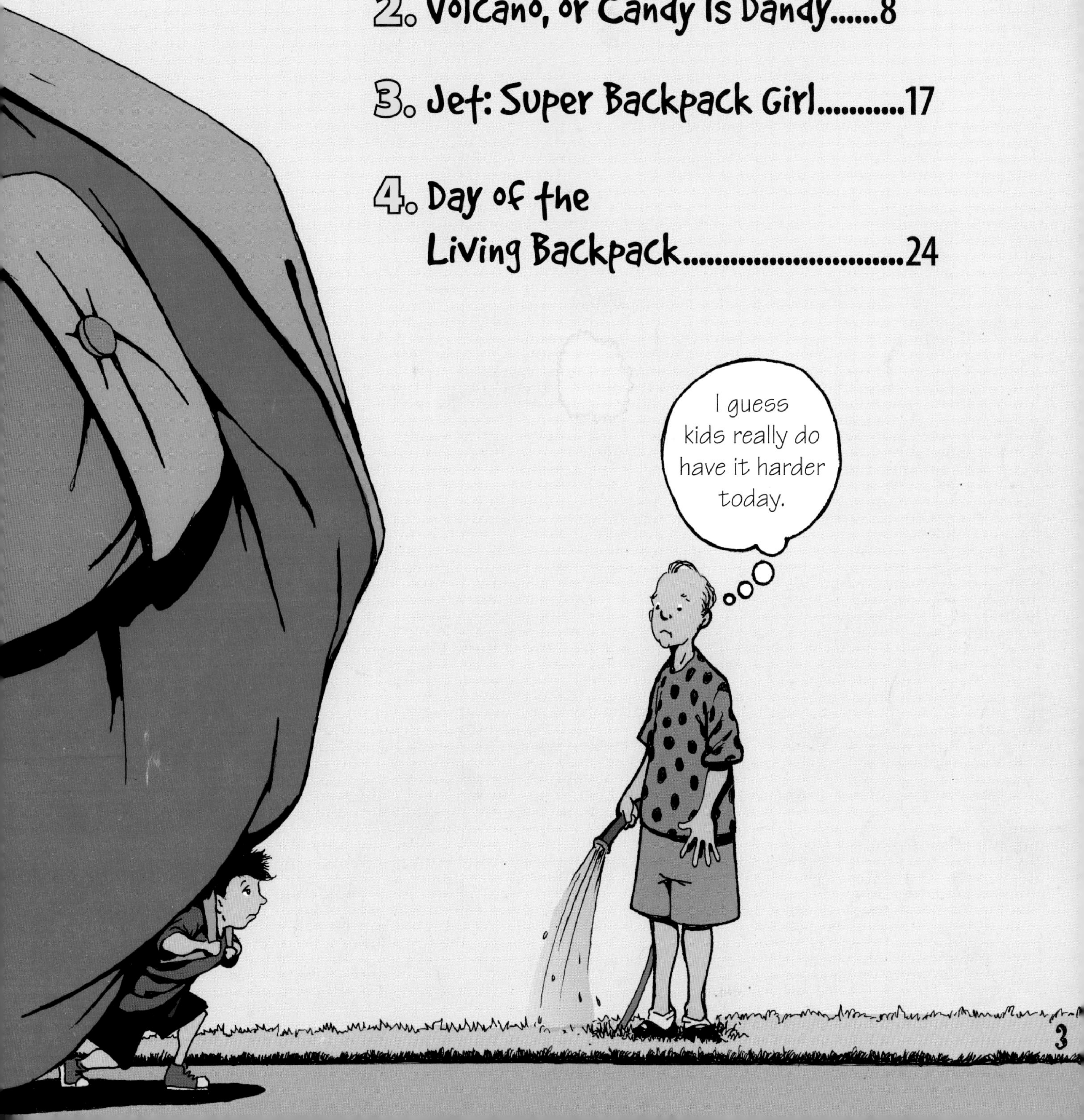
I guess kids really do have it harder today.

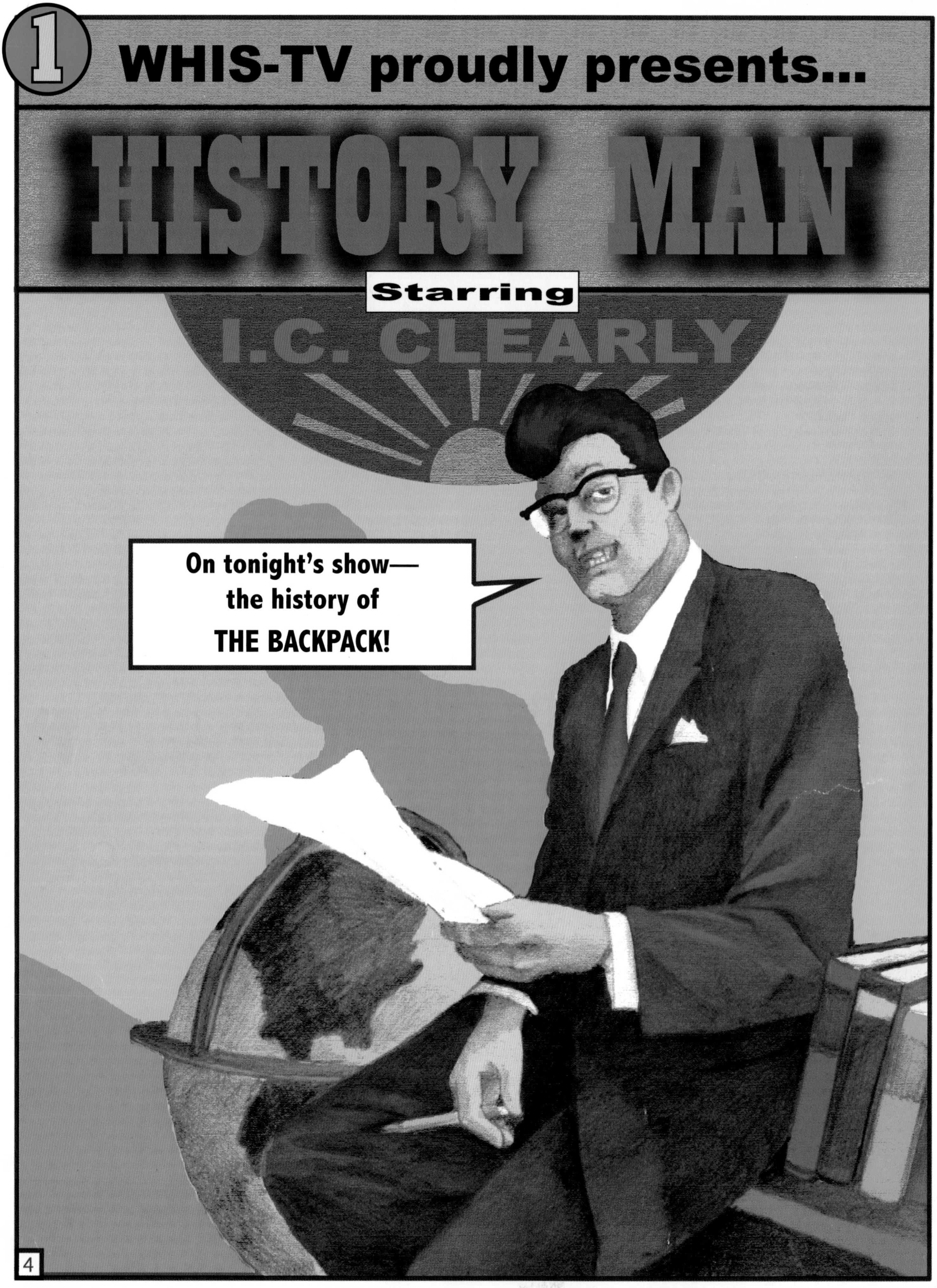
1
WHIS-TV proudly presents...
HISTORY MAN
Starring
I.C. CLEARLY
On tonight's show— the history of THE BACKPACK!

Historians believe the first backpack was created by a caveman named Roscoe. He wrapped up his things in fur and swung the pack over his back. Unfortunately his friends thought he was being attacked by a beaver, and they pounded him with sticks.

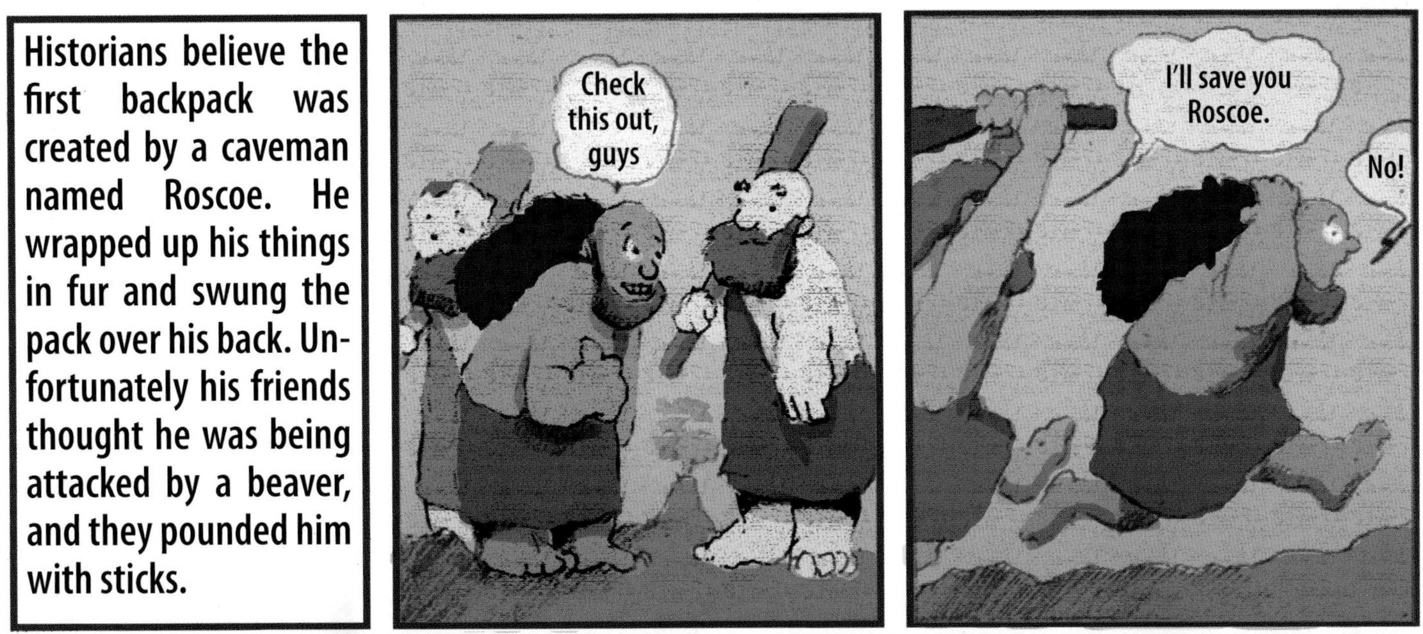
Check this out, guys
I'll save you Roscoe.
No!

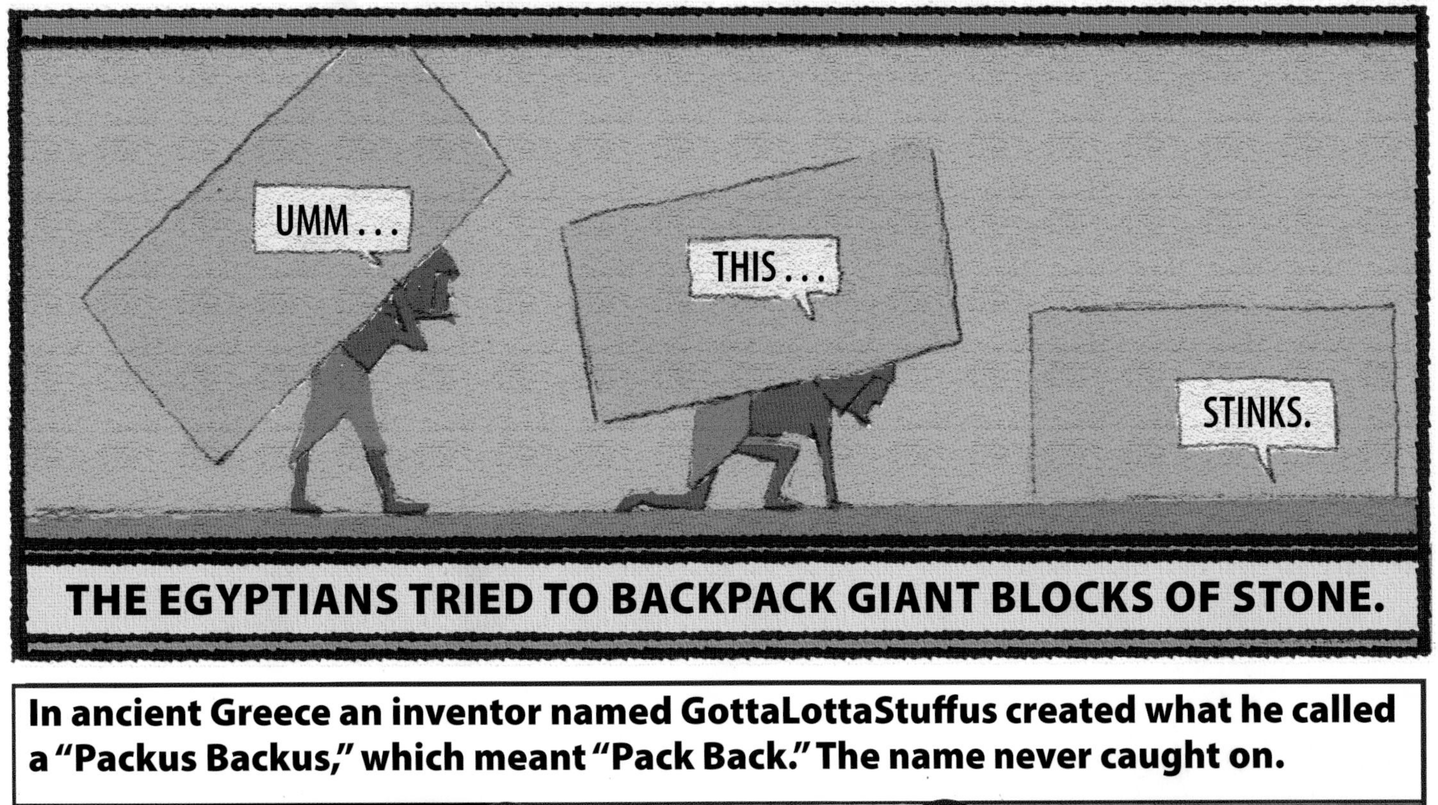
UMM . . .
THIS . . .
STINKS.

THE EGYPTIANS TRIED TO BACKPACK GIANT BLOCKS OF STONE.

In ancient Greece an inventor named GottaLottaStuffus created what he called a "Packus Backus," which meant "Pack Back." The name never caught on.

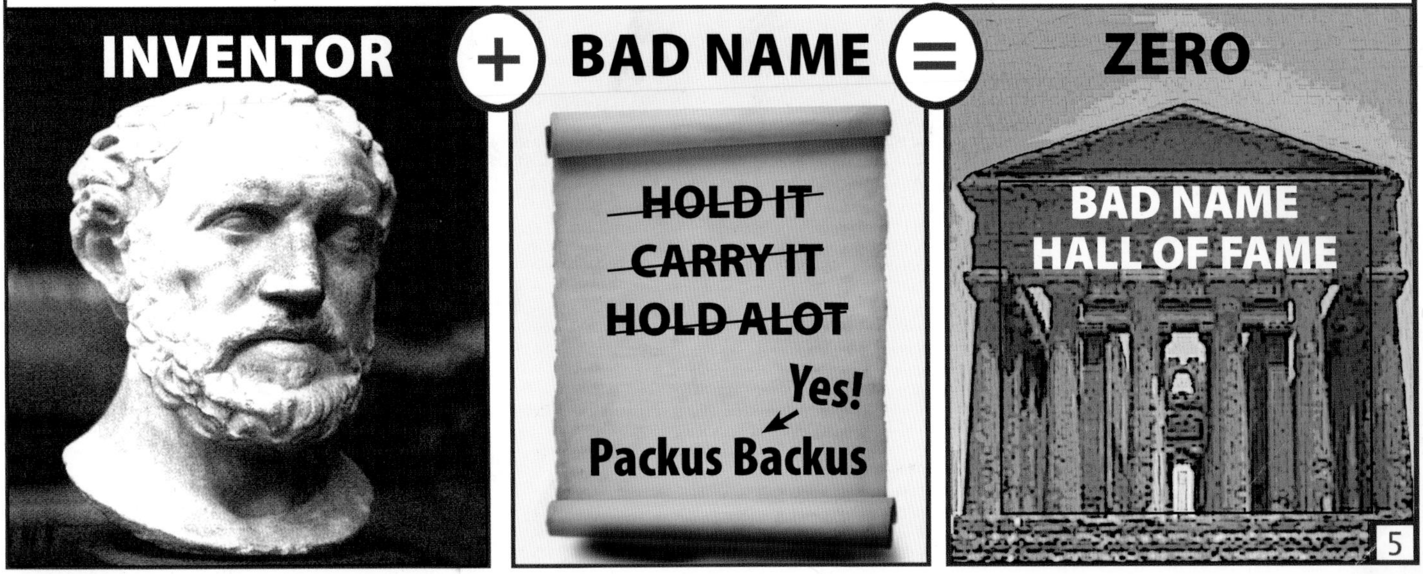
INVENTOR
+
BAD NAME
=
ZERO
~~HOLD IT~~
~~CARRY IT~~
~~HOLD ALOT~~
Yes!
Packus Backus
BAD NAME HALL OF FAME

WHITEY SHORTS

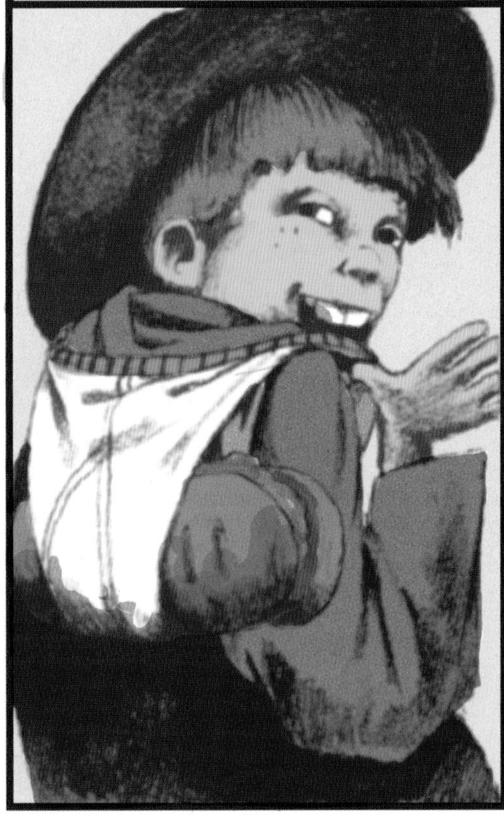

In 1883 a young man named Whitey Shorts created a backpack by using his underwear. Whitey slipped his arms into the leg holes. Finding it comfortable, he put his lunch in the underwear and went to school. His principal was not amused.

MRS. LACKAHUMOR

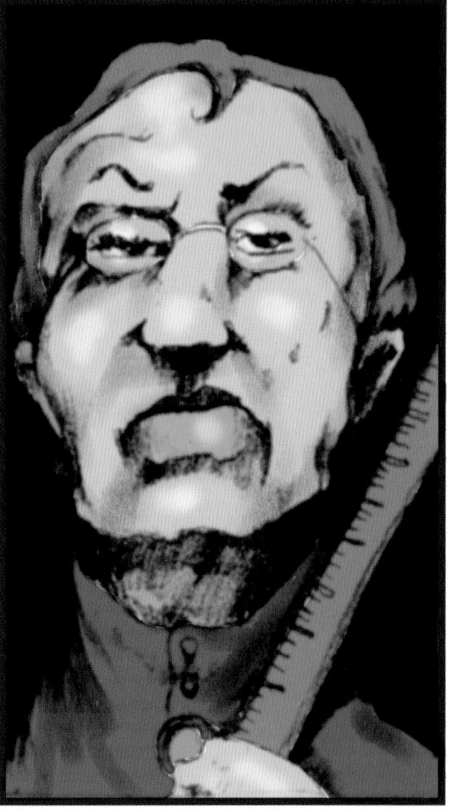

In the 1940s kids looked like this. They carried their books using a thick rubber strap with a hook on each end.

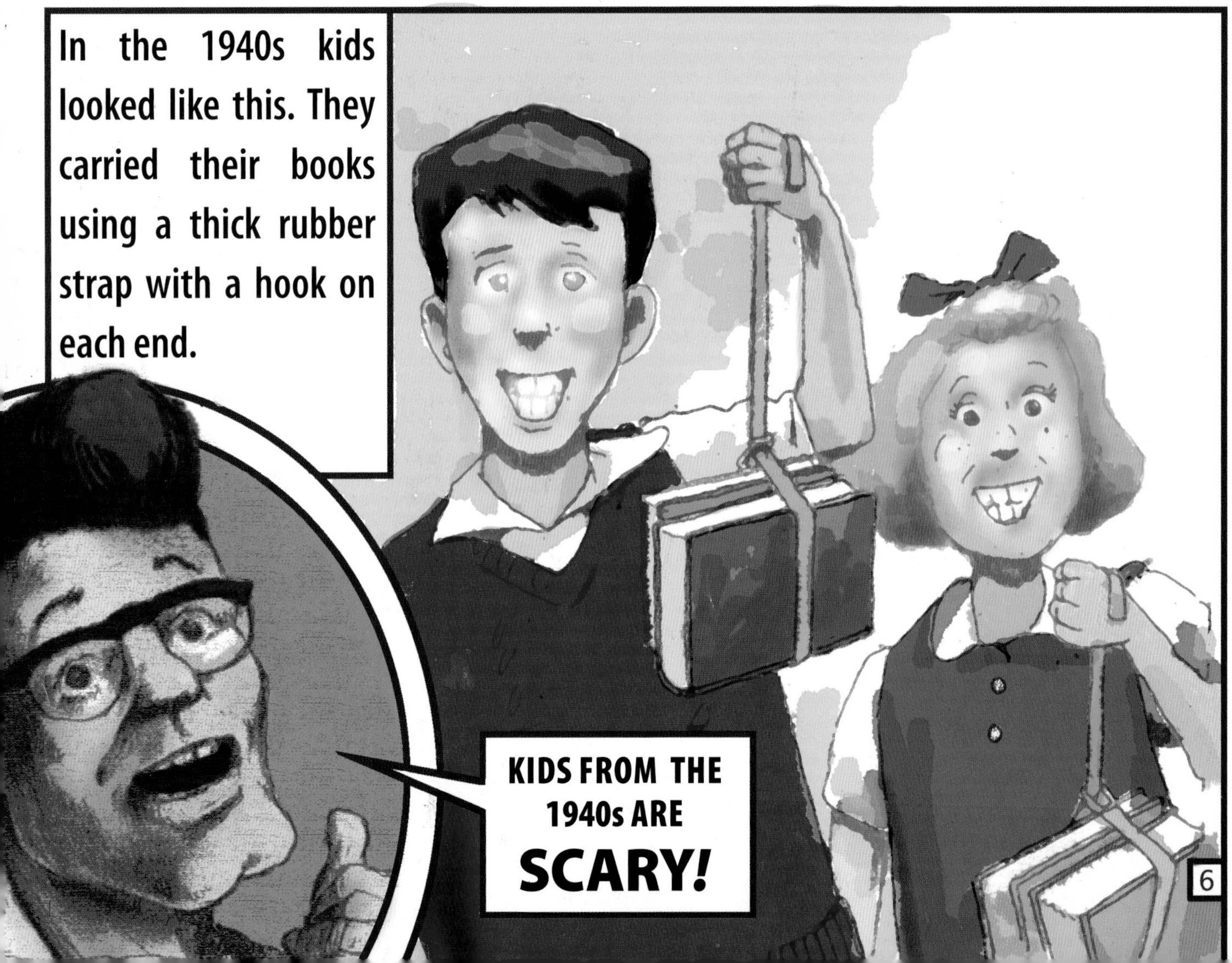
KIDS FROM THE 1940s ARE SCARY!

Today's modern backpack is a wonder to behold. The child of the 21st century no longer struggles on the way to school. Why? Because kids today have their moms carry their stuff!

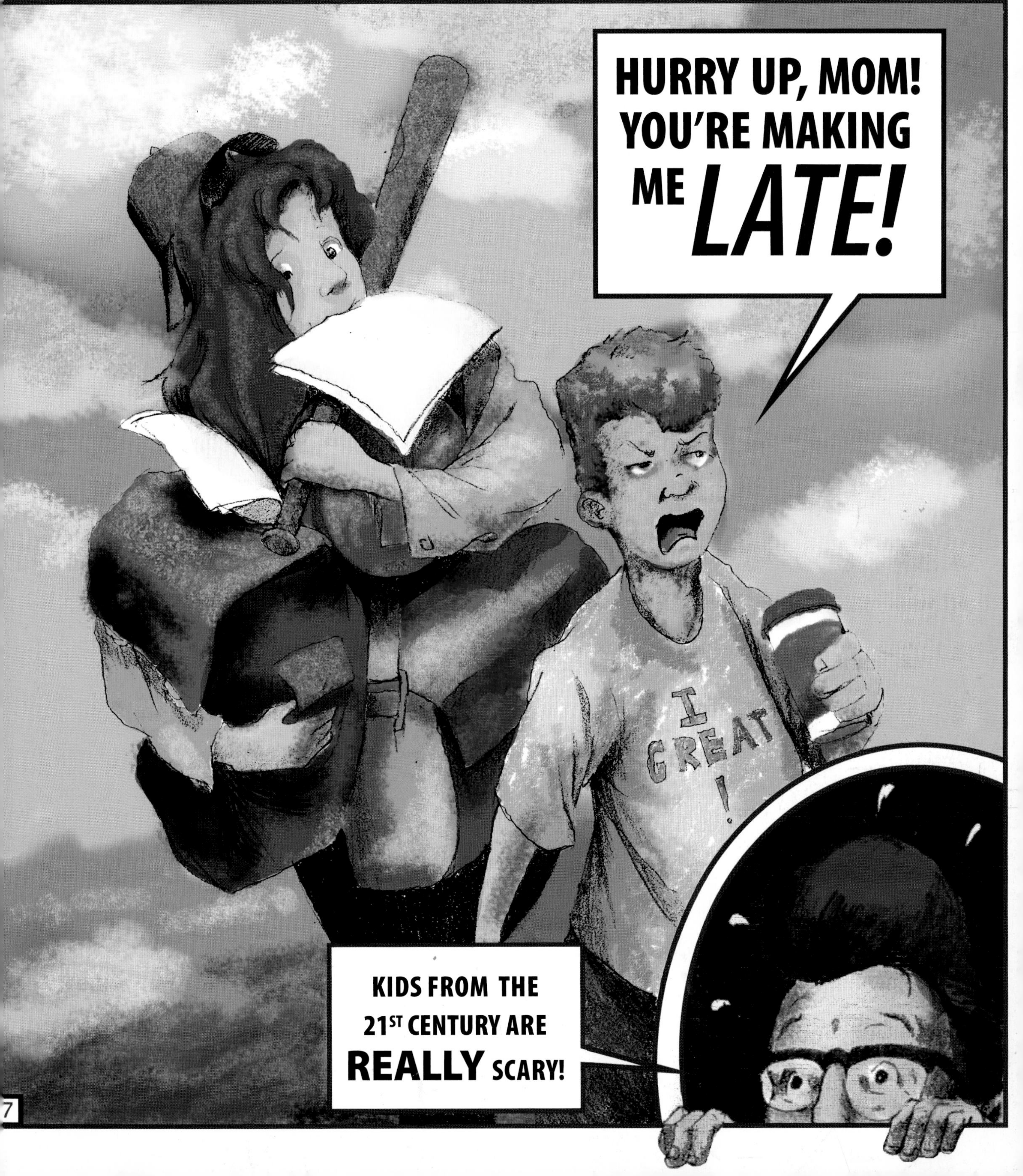
HURRY UP, MOM! YOU'RE MAKING ME LATE!
I GREAT!
KIDS FROM THE 21ST CENTURY ARE REALLY SCARY!

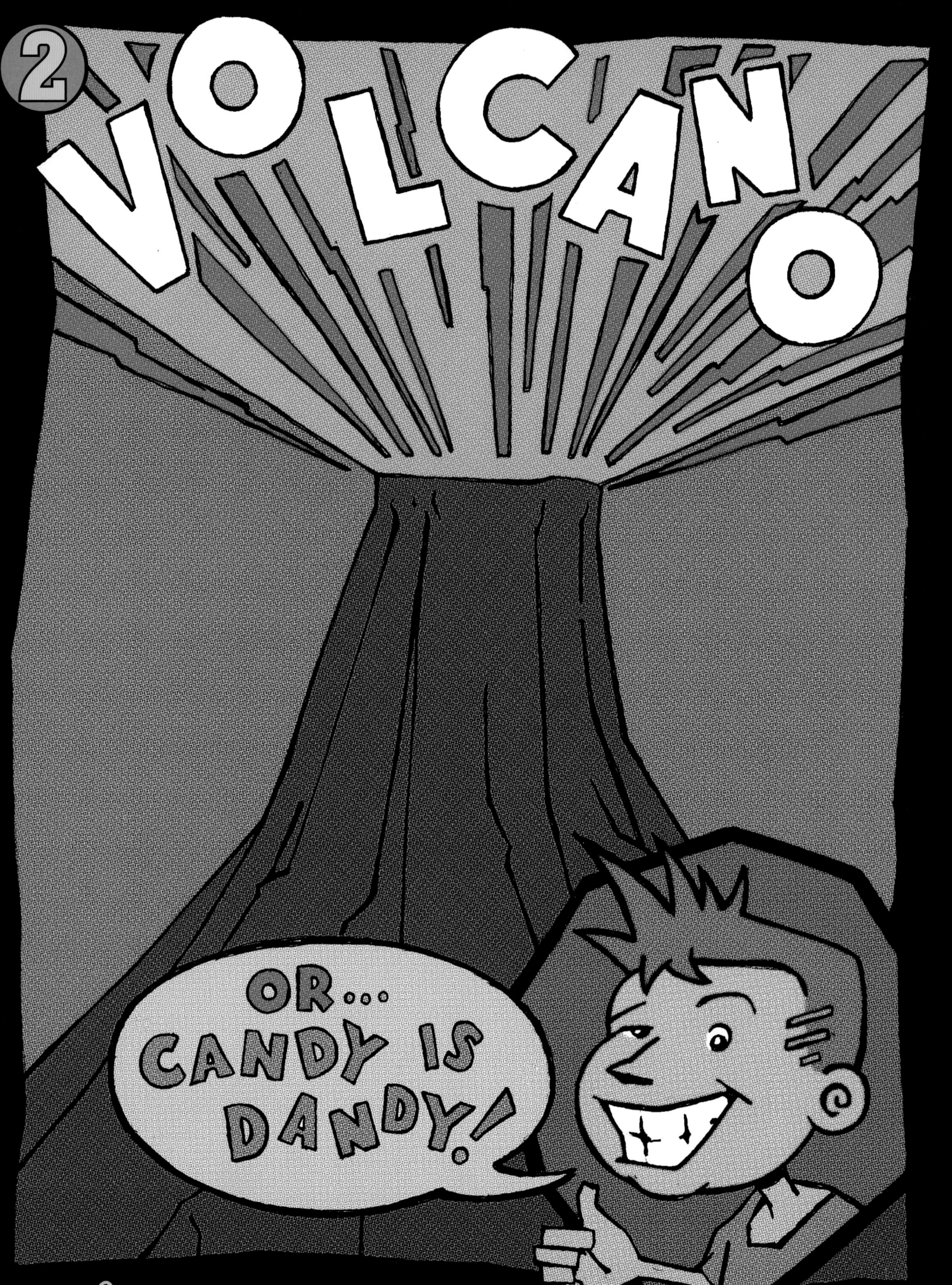
2
VOLCANO
OR...
CANDY IS DANDY!

AFTER WEEKS OF WORK, BRENDAN DISCOVERED THAT HIS VOLCANO SCIENCE-FAIR PROJECT DIDN'T GO KA-BOOM!

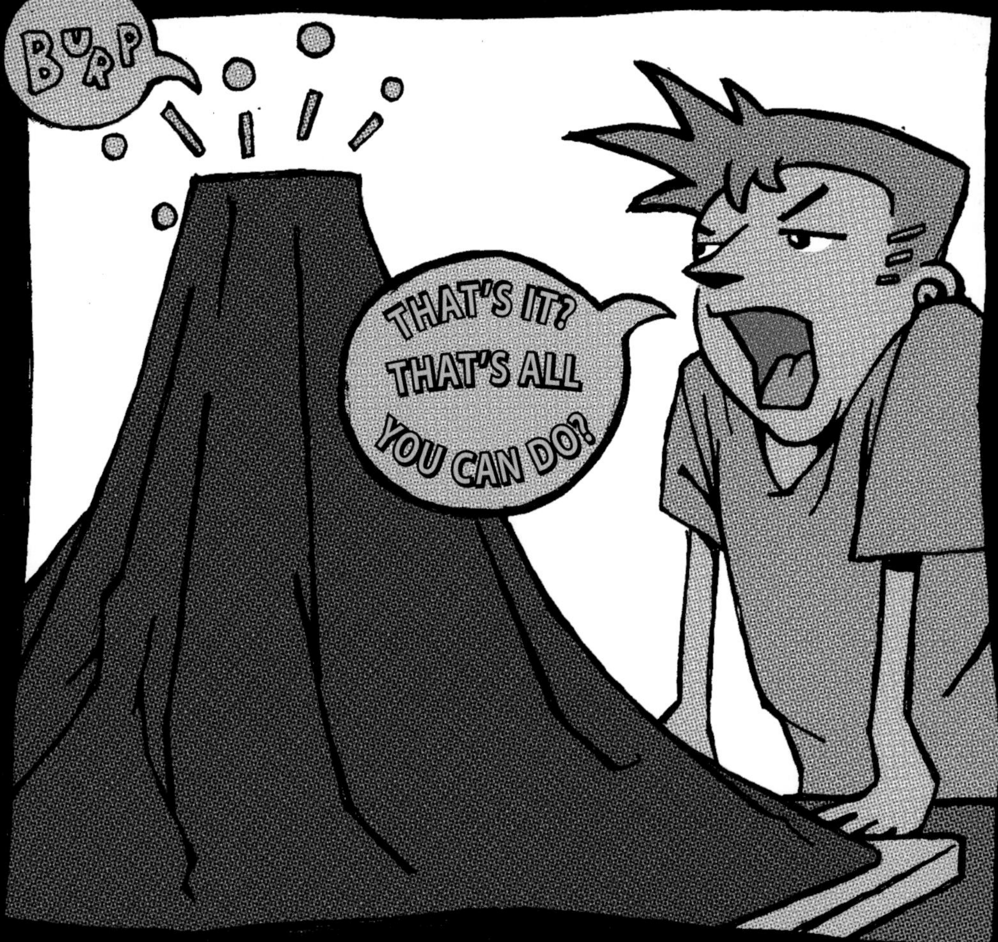
BURP
THAT'S IT? THAT'S ALL YOU CAN DO?

THERE WAS NOTHING MORE HE COULD DO. TOMORROW WAS THE DAY OF THE SCIENCE FAIR, SO BRENDAN PACKED UP HIS SCHOOL SUPPLIES.

HE PACKED UP . . .

12 VOLCANO BOOKS
1 CALCULATOR
3 CHEWED-UP PENCILS
1 BINDER
2 NOTEBOOKS
1 PAINT SET
1 STAPLE REMOVER
1 PENCIL SHARPENER
1 COMPASS SET
1 OLD BIT OF CANDY WITH SOME HAIR AND LINT STUCK TO IT

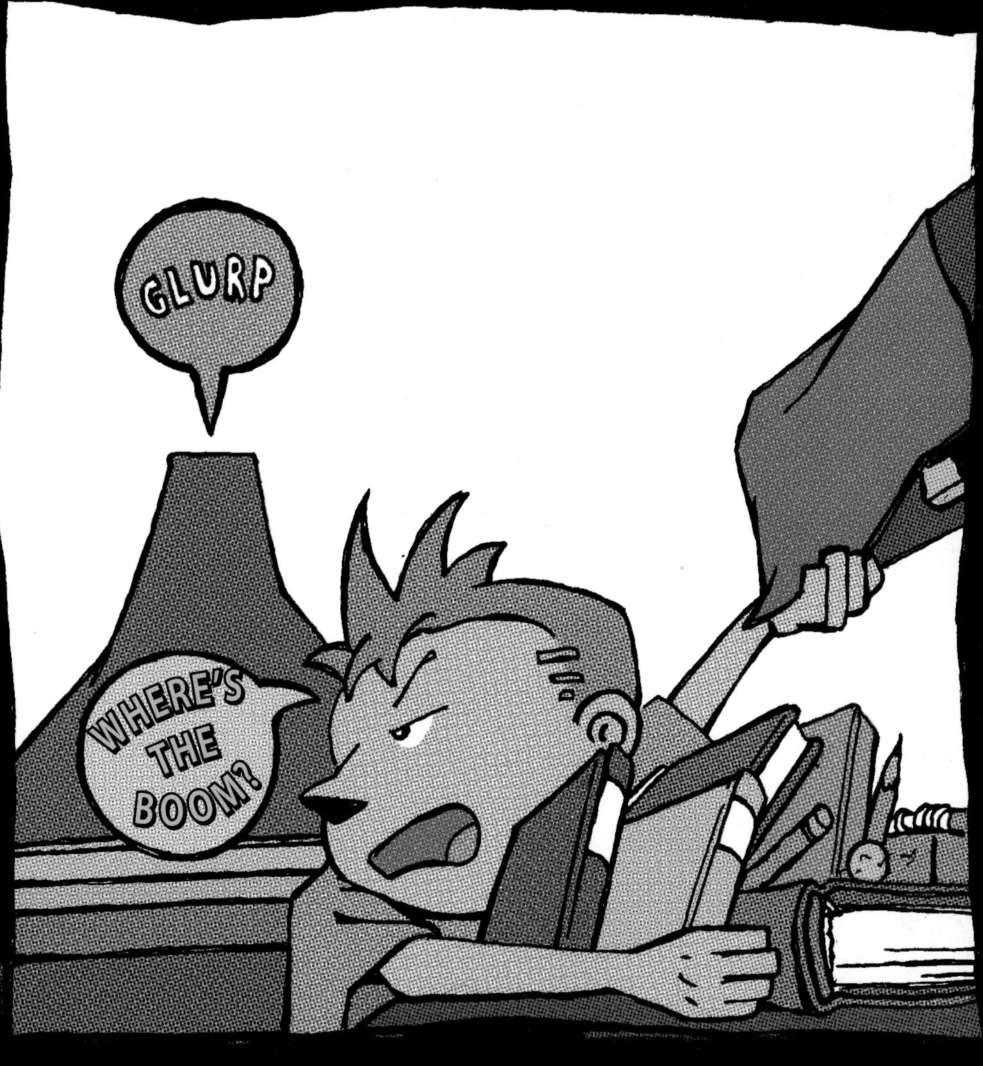
GLURP
WHERE'S THE BOOM?

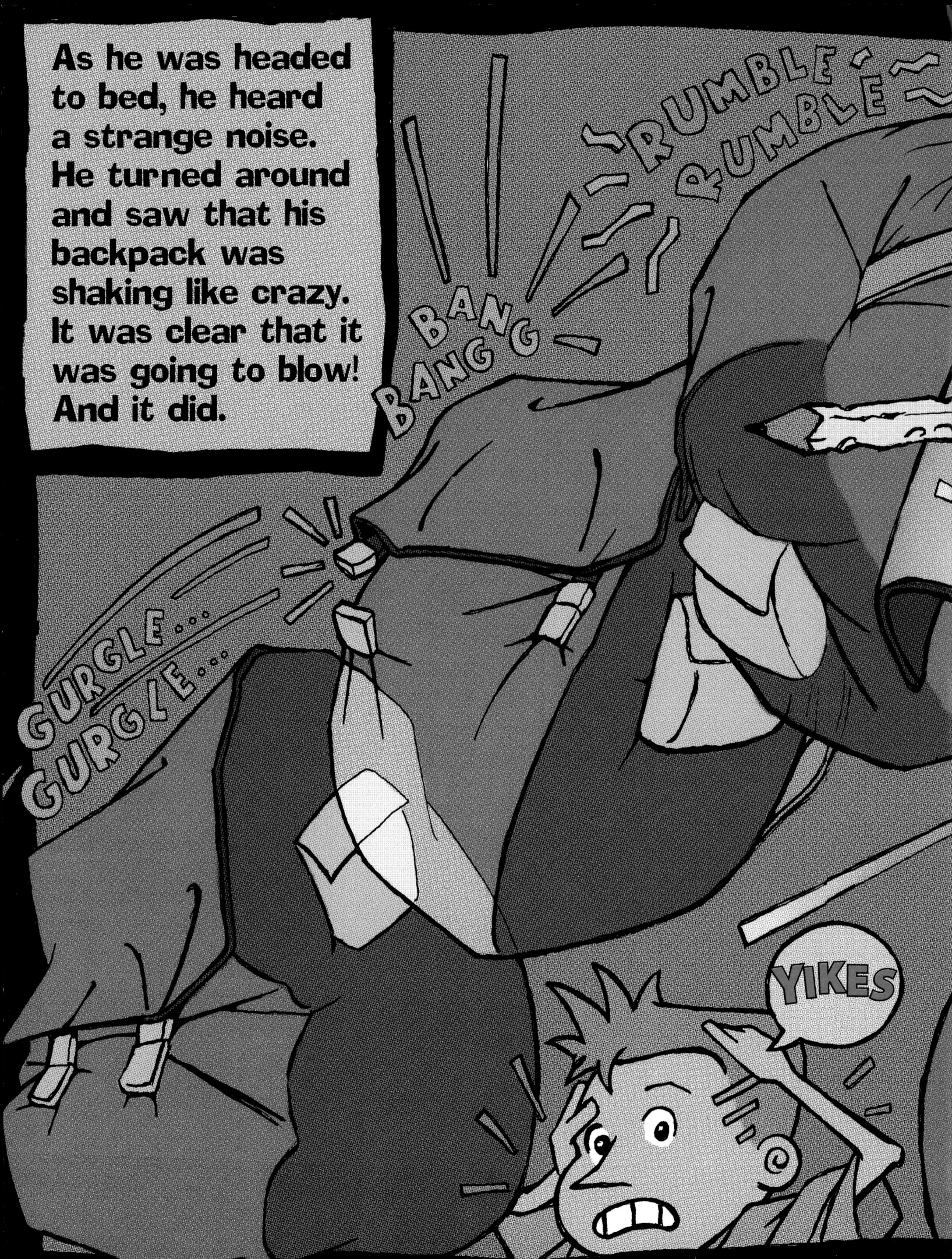
As he was headed to bed, he heard a strange noise. He turned around and saw that his backpack was shaking like crazy. It was clear that it was going to blow! And it did.
RUMBLE
RUMBLE
BANG
BANG
GURGLE...
GURGLE...
YIKES

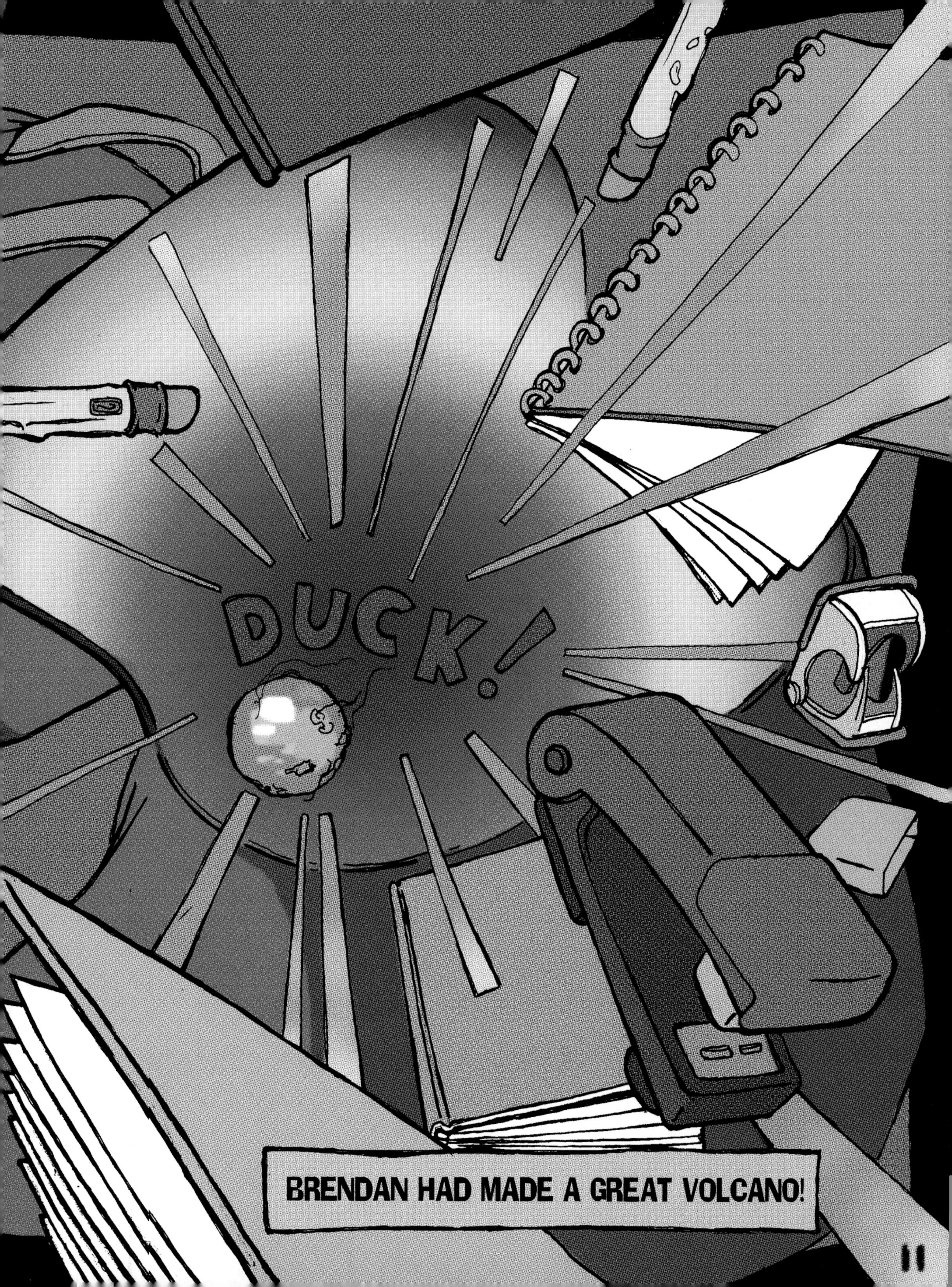
DUCK!
BRENDAN HAD MADE A GREAT VOLCANO!

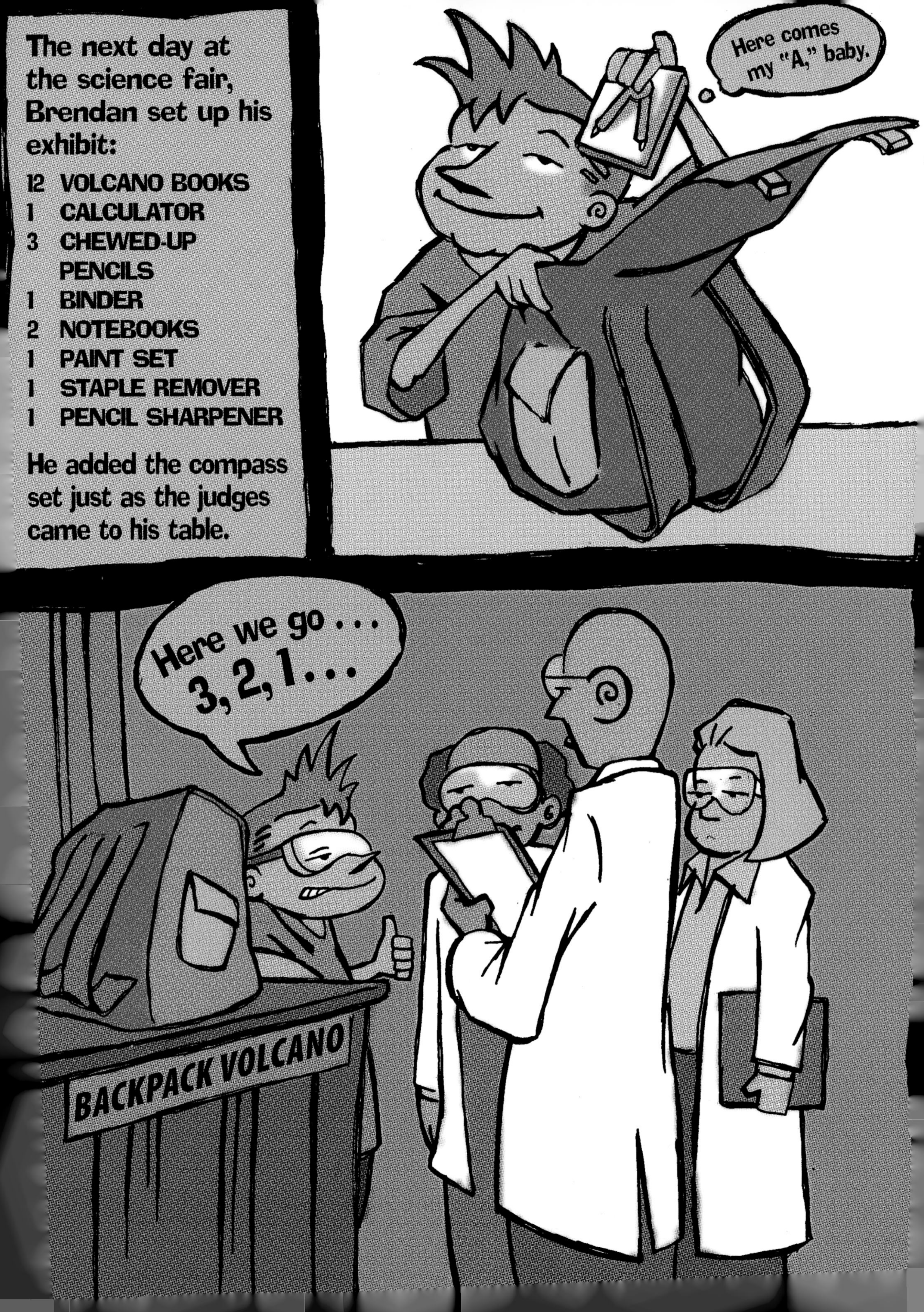
The next day at the science fair, Brendan set up his exhibit:
12 VOLCANO BOOKS
1 CALCULATOR
3 CHEWED-UP PENCILS
1 BINDER
2 NOTEBOOKS
1 PAINT SET
1 STAPLE REMOVER
1 PENCIL SHARPENER
He added the compass set just as the judges came to his table.
Here comes my "A," baby.
Here we go . . . 3, 2, 1 . . .
BACKPACK VOLCANO

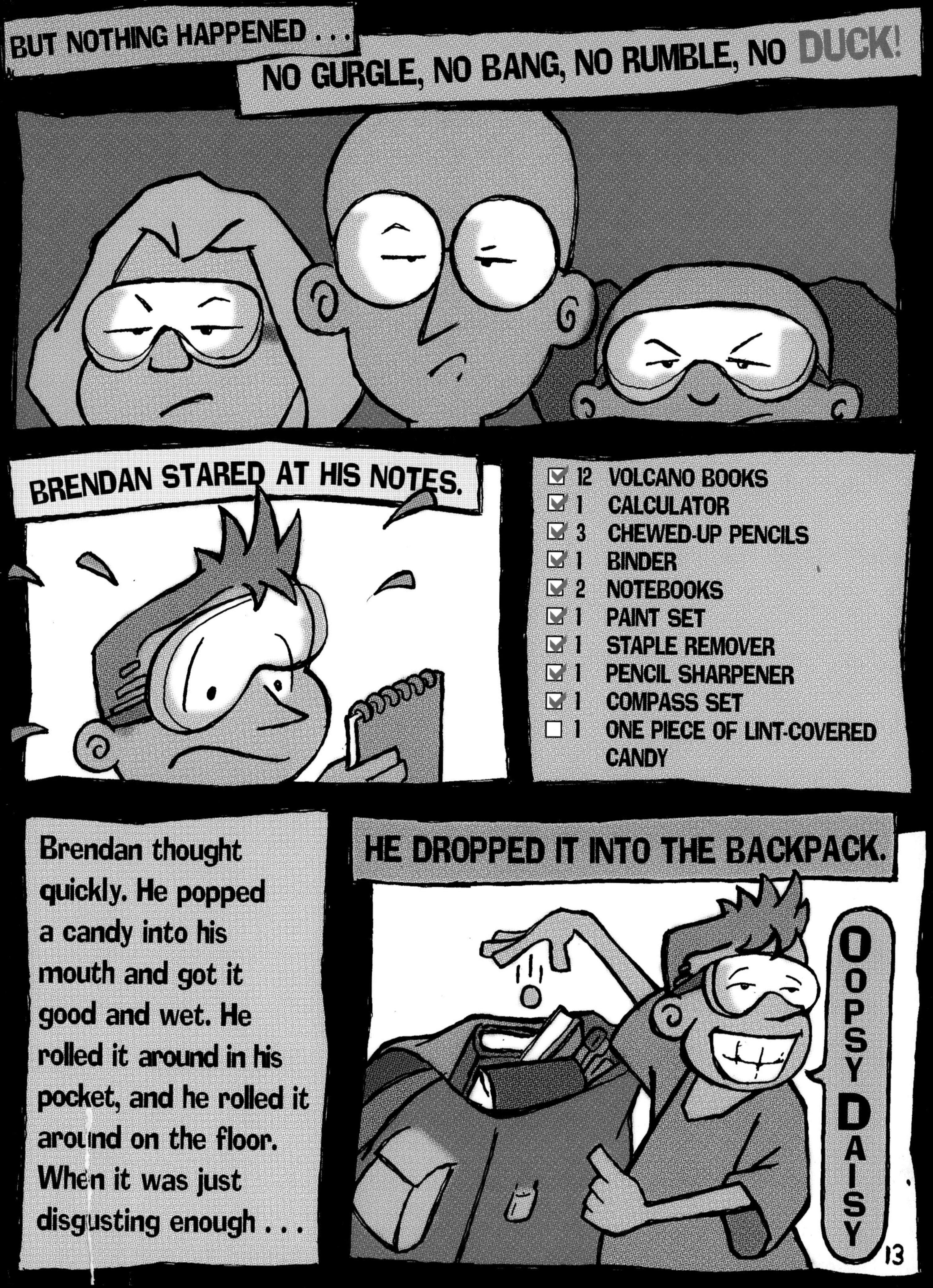
BUT NOTHING HAPPENED . . .
NO GURGLE, NO BANG, NO RUMBLE, NO DUCK!
BRENDAN STARED AT HIS NOTES.
☑ 12 VOLCANO BOOKS
☑ 1 CALCULATOR
☑ 3 CHEWED-UP PENCILS
☑ 1 BINDER
☑ 2 NOTEBOOKS
☑ 1 PAINT SET
☑ 1 STAPLE REMOVER
☑ 1 PENCIL SHARPENER
☑ 1 COMPASS SET
☐ 1 ONE PIECE OF LINT-COVERED CANDY
Brendan thought quickly. He popped a candy into his mouth and got it good and wet. He rolled it around in his pocket, and he rolled it around on the floor. When it was just disgusting enough . . .
HE DROPPED IT INTO THE BACKPACK.
OOPSY DAISY

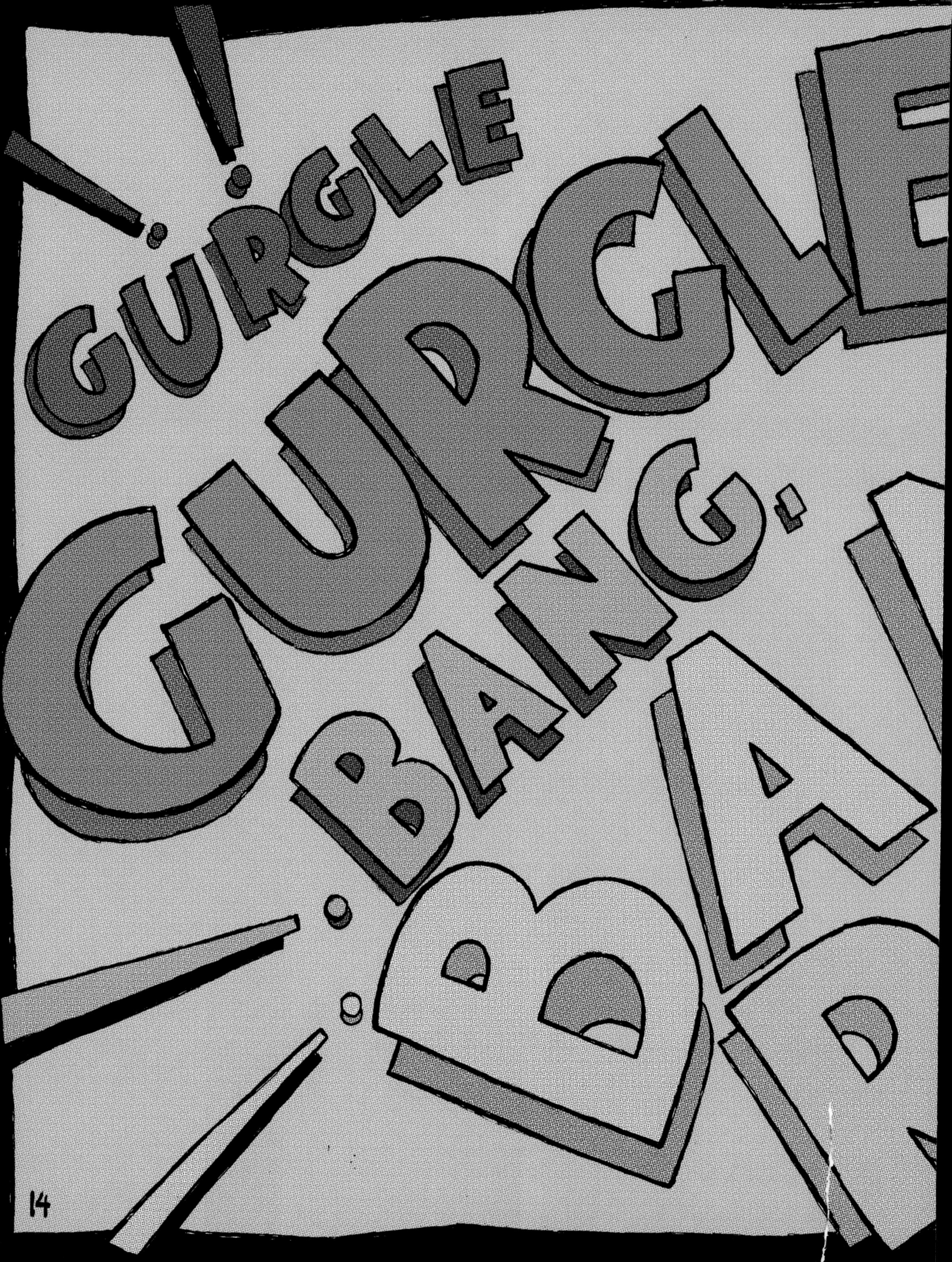
GURGLE!
GURGLE
BANG!
BA

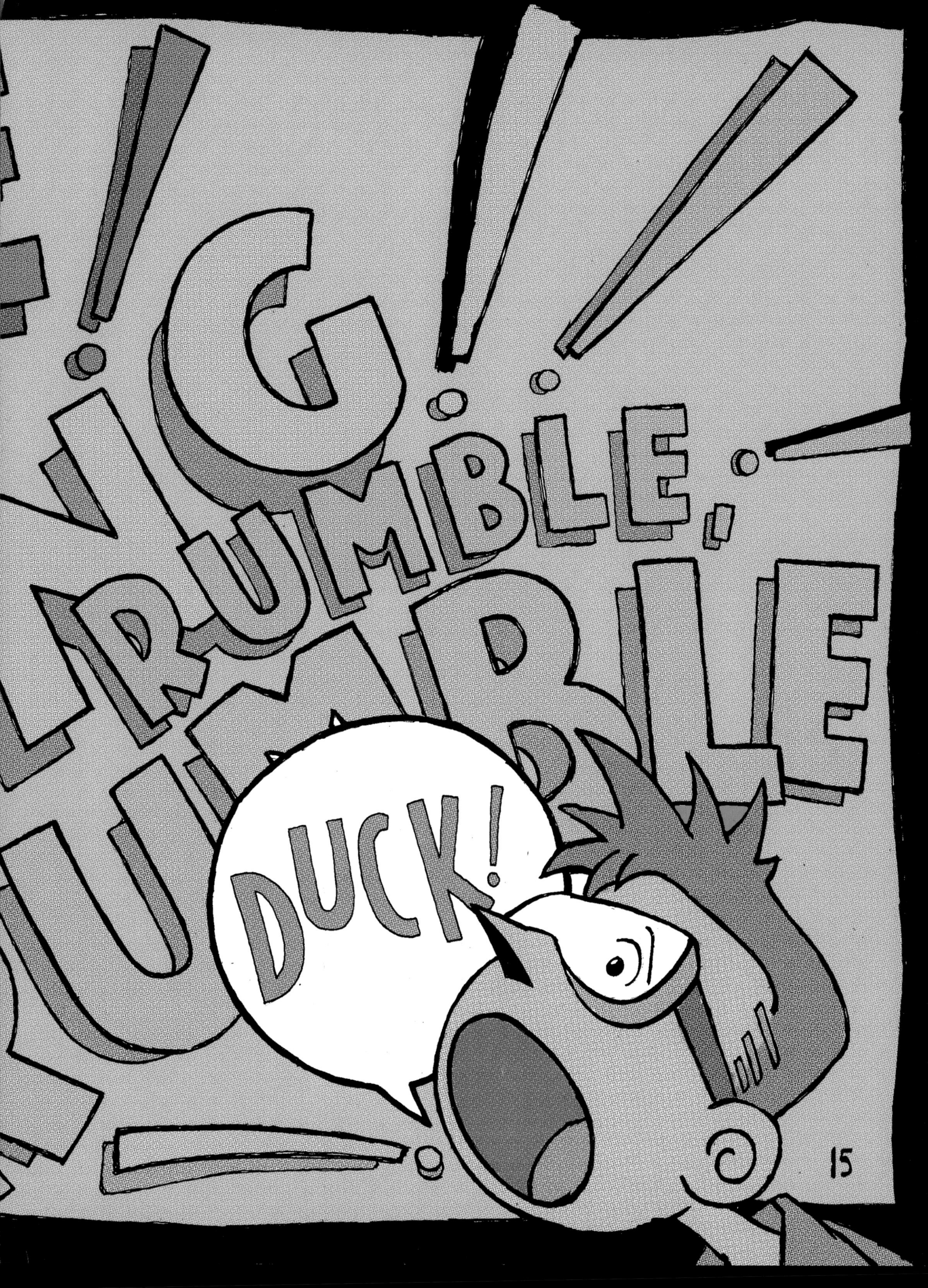
G!!
RUMBLE,
RUMBLE
DUCK!

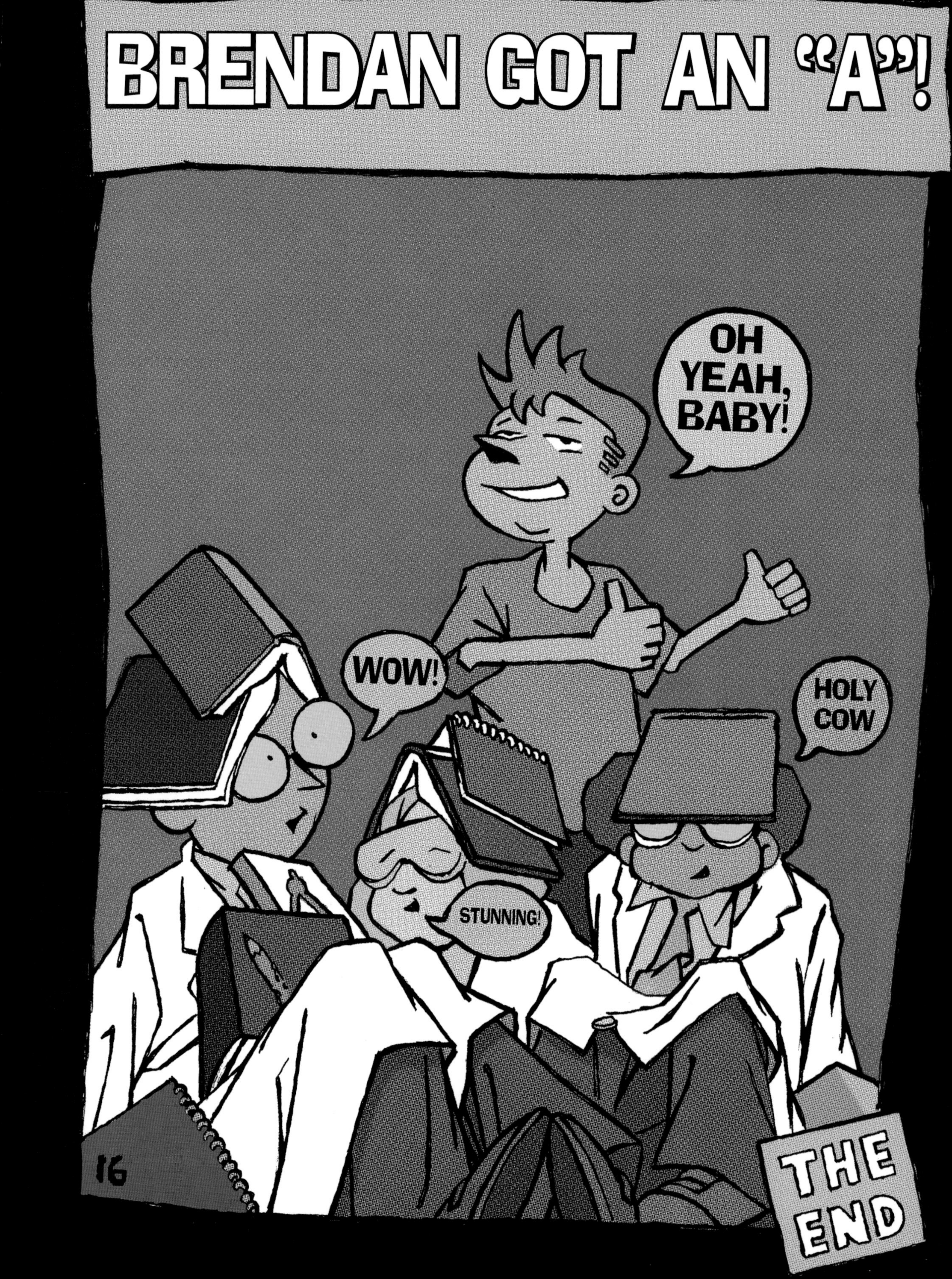
BRENDAN GOT AN "A"!
OH YEAH, BABY!
WOW!
HOLY COW
STUNNING!
THE END

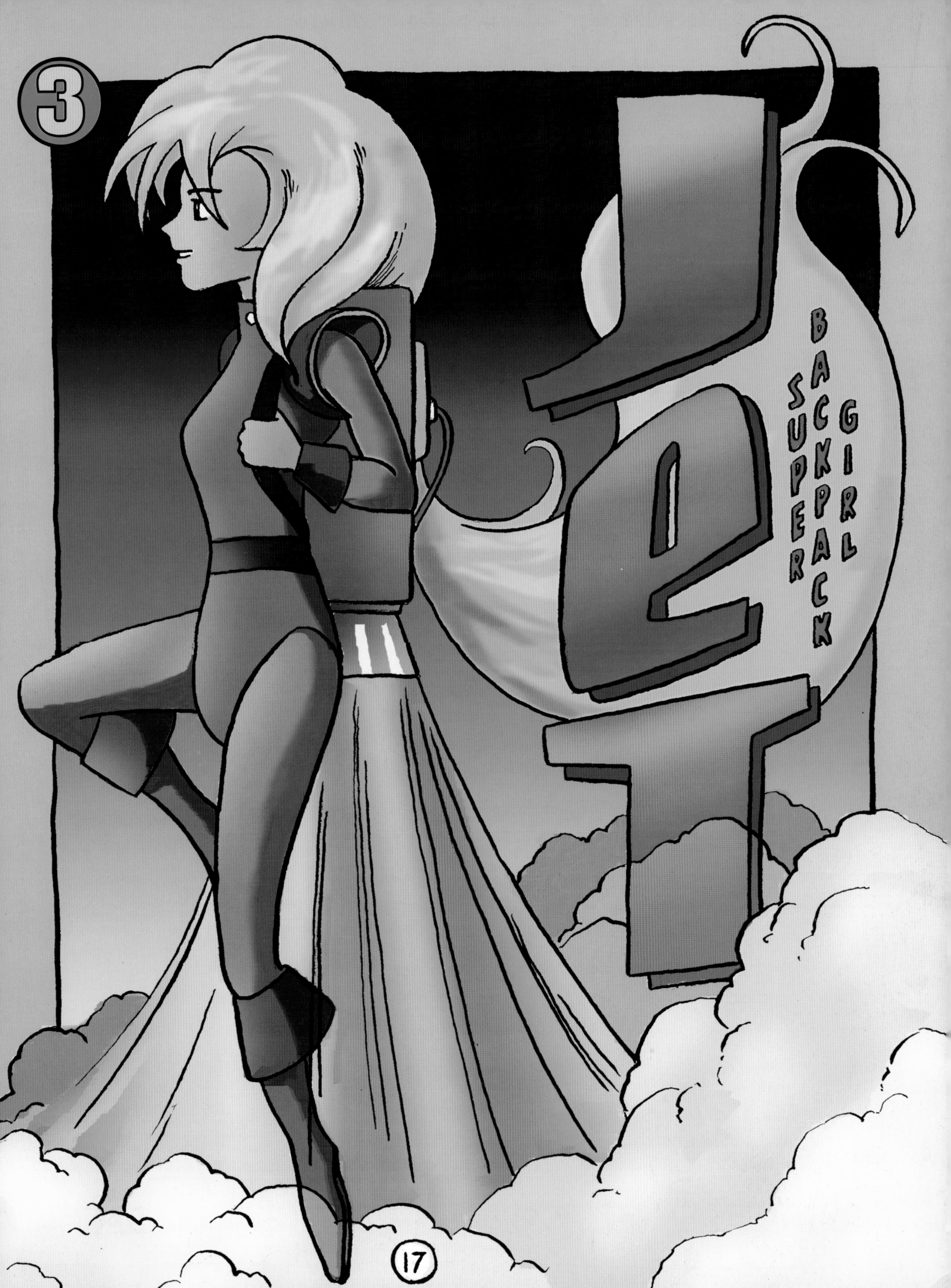
3
JET
SUPER BACKPACK GIRL

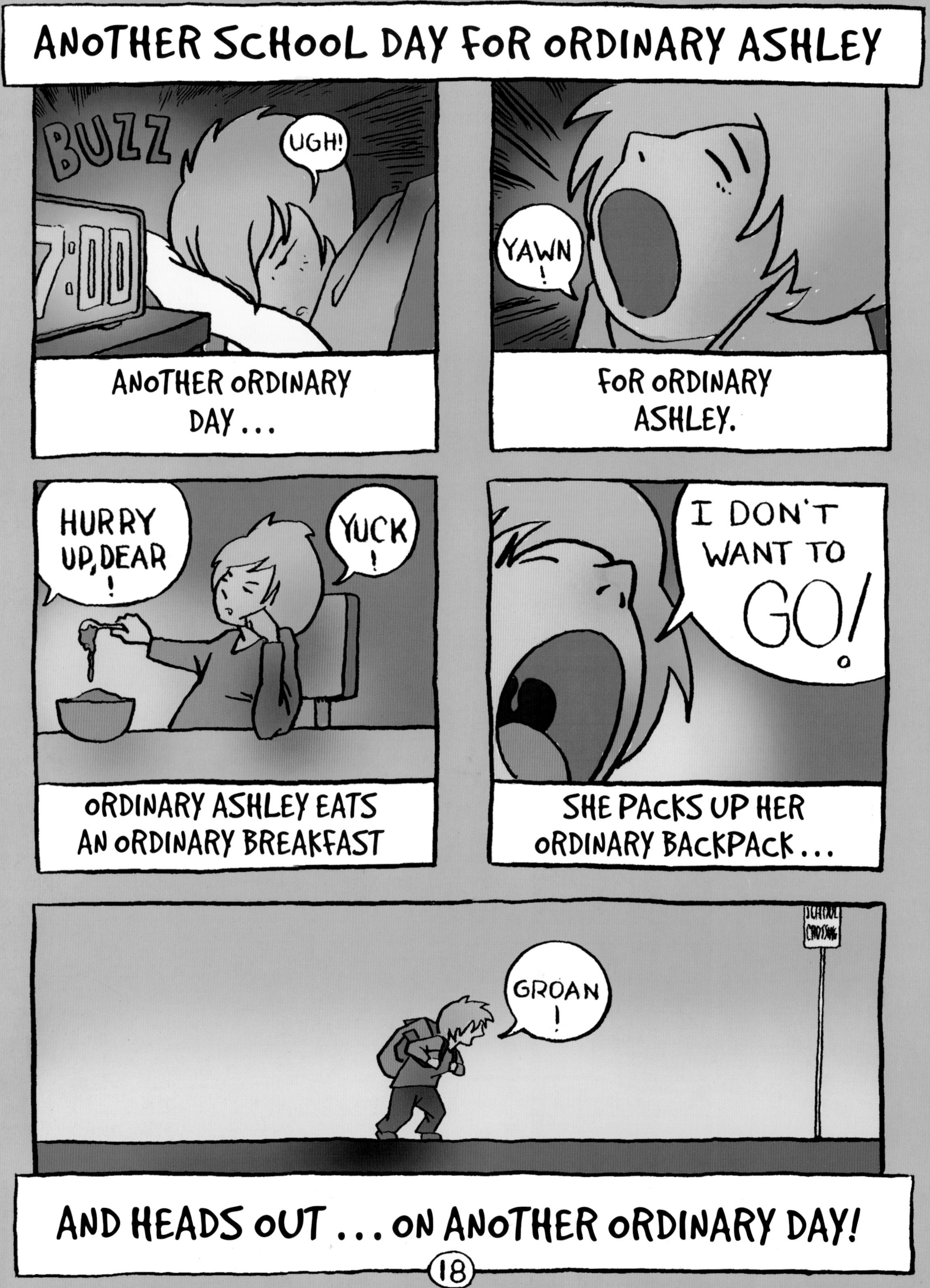
ANOTHER SCHOOL DAY FOR ORDINARY ASHLEY
BUZZ
7:00
UGH!
ANOTHER ORDINARY DAY . . .
YAWN!
FOR ORDINARY ASHLEY.
HURRY UP, DEAR!
YUCK!
ORDINARY ASHLEY EATS AN ORDINARY BREAKFAST
I DON'T WANT TO GO!
SHE PACKS UP HER ORDINARY BACKPACK . . .
GROAN!
AND HEADS OUT . . . ON ANOTHER ORDINARY DAY!

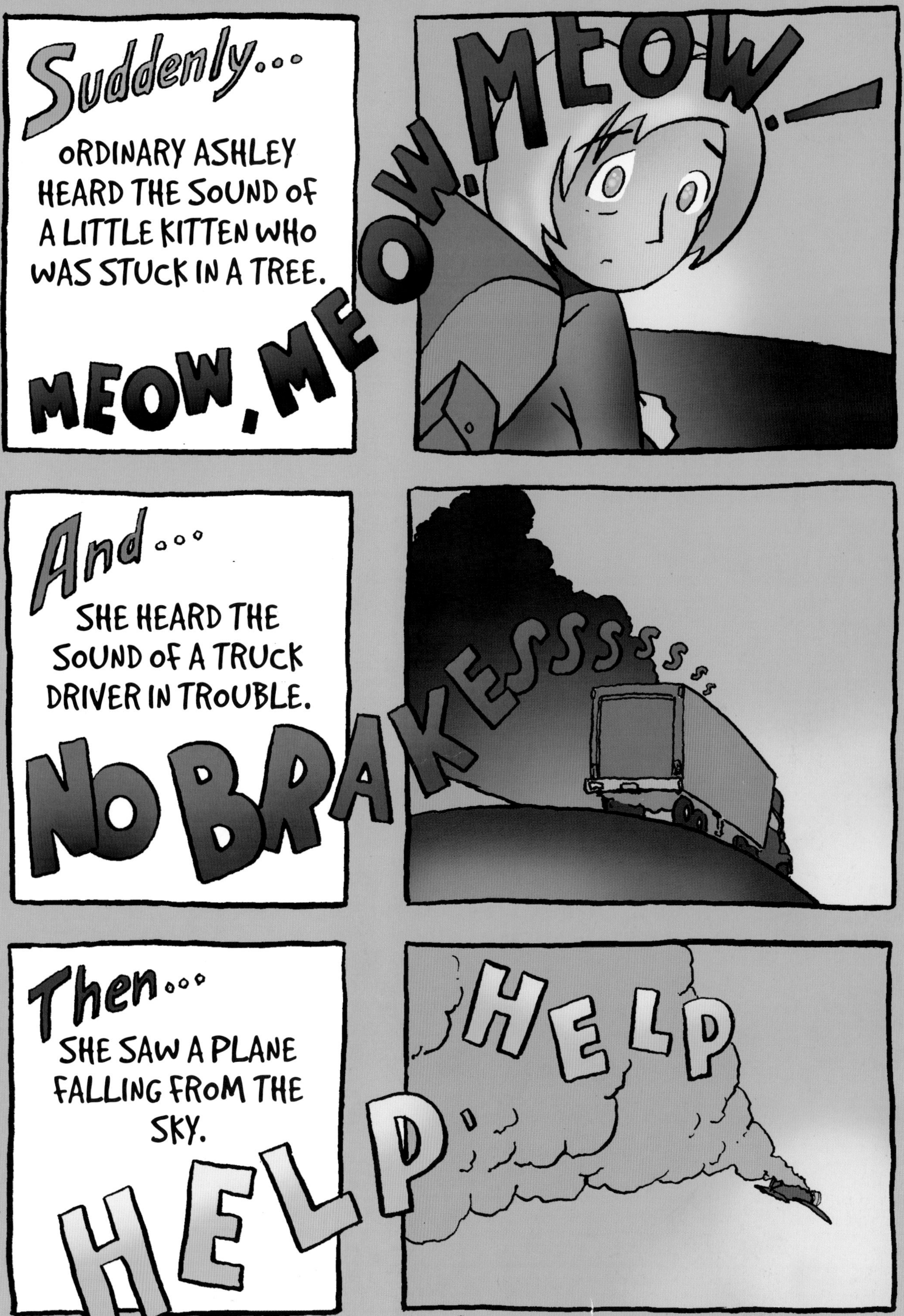
Suddenly...
ORDINARY ASHLEY HEARD THE SOUND OF A LITTLE KITTEN WHO WAS STUCK IN A TREE.
MEOW, MEOW, MEOW, MEOW.!
And...
SHE HEARD THE SOUND OF A TRUCK DRIVER IN TROUBLE.
NO BRAKESSSSSSSS
Then...
SHE SAW A PLANE FALLING FROM THE SKY.
HELP. HELP

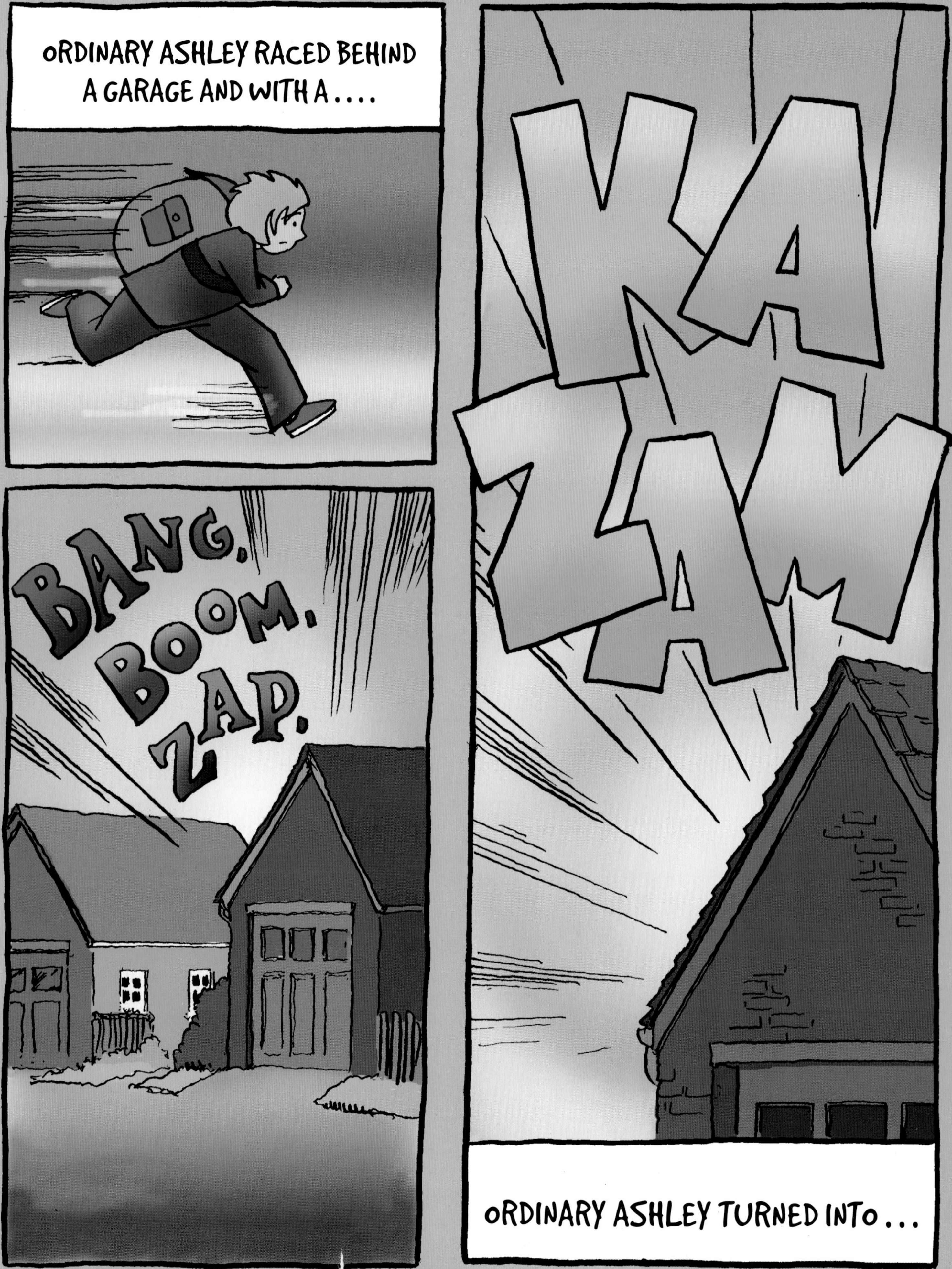
ORDINARY ASHLEY RACED BEHIND A GARAGE AND WITH A....
BANG, BOOM, ZAP,
KA ZAM
ORDINARY ASHLEY TURNED INTO...

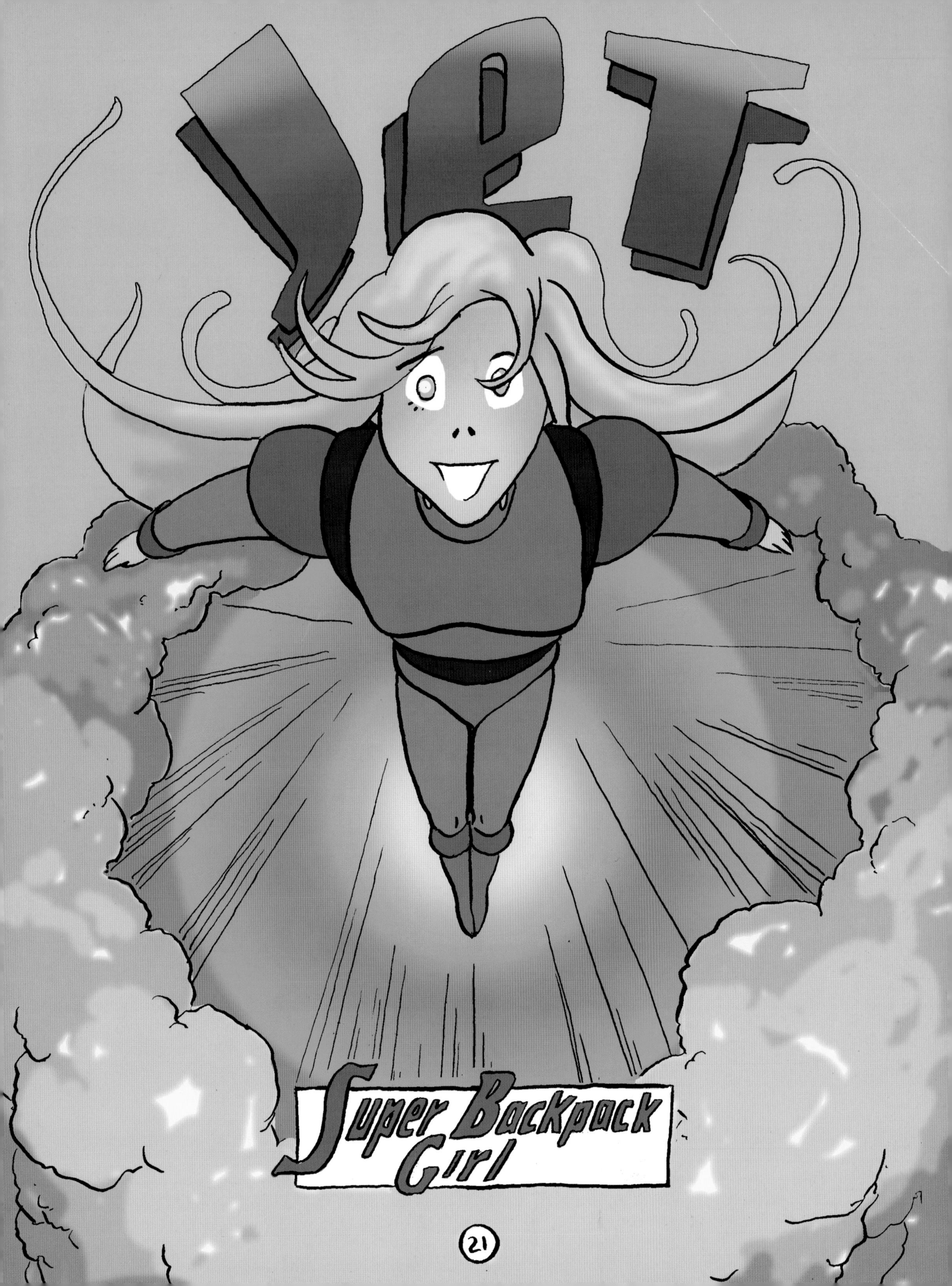
Super Backpack Girl

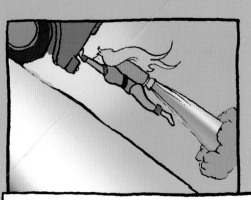

FIRST THE AMAZING JET STOPPED THE OUT-OF-CONTROL TRUCK!

THEN SHE CAUGHT THE DAMAGED PLANE AND LOWERED IT DOWN TO EARTH.

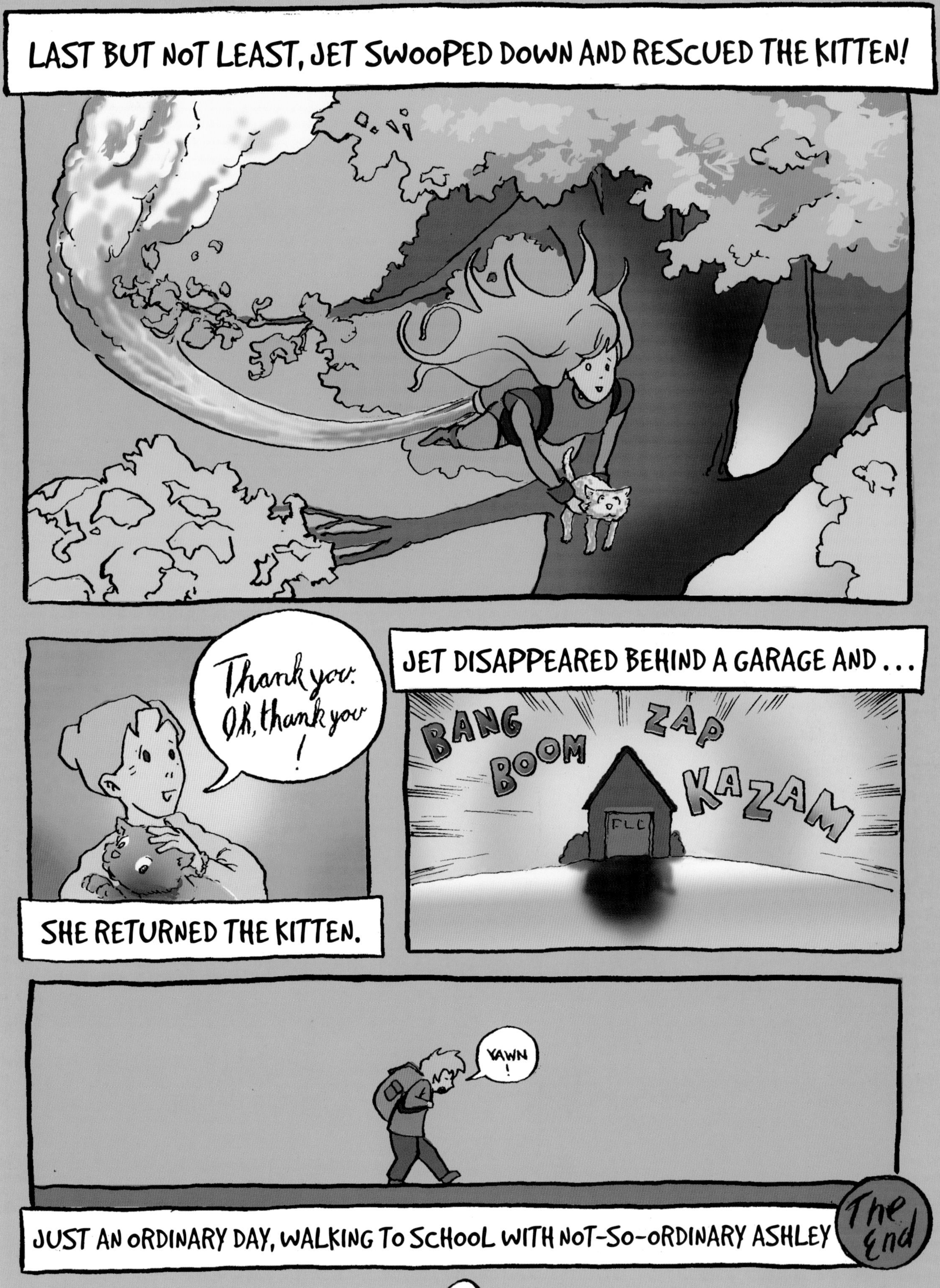

LAST BUT NOT LEAST, JET SWOOPED DOWN AND RESCUED THE KITTEN!
Thank you. Oh, thank you!
SHE RETURNED THE KITTEN.
JET DISAPPEARED BEHIND A GARAGE AND . . .
BANG
BOOM
ZAP
KAZAM
YAWN!
JUST AN ORDINARY DAY, WALKING TO SCHOOL WITH NOT-SO-ORDINARY ASHLEY
The End

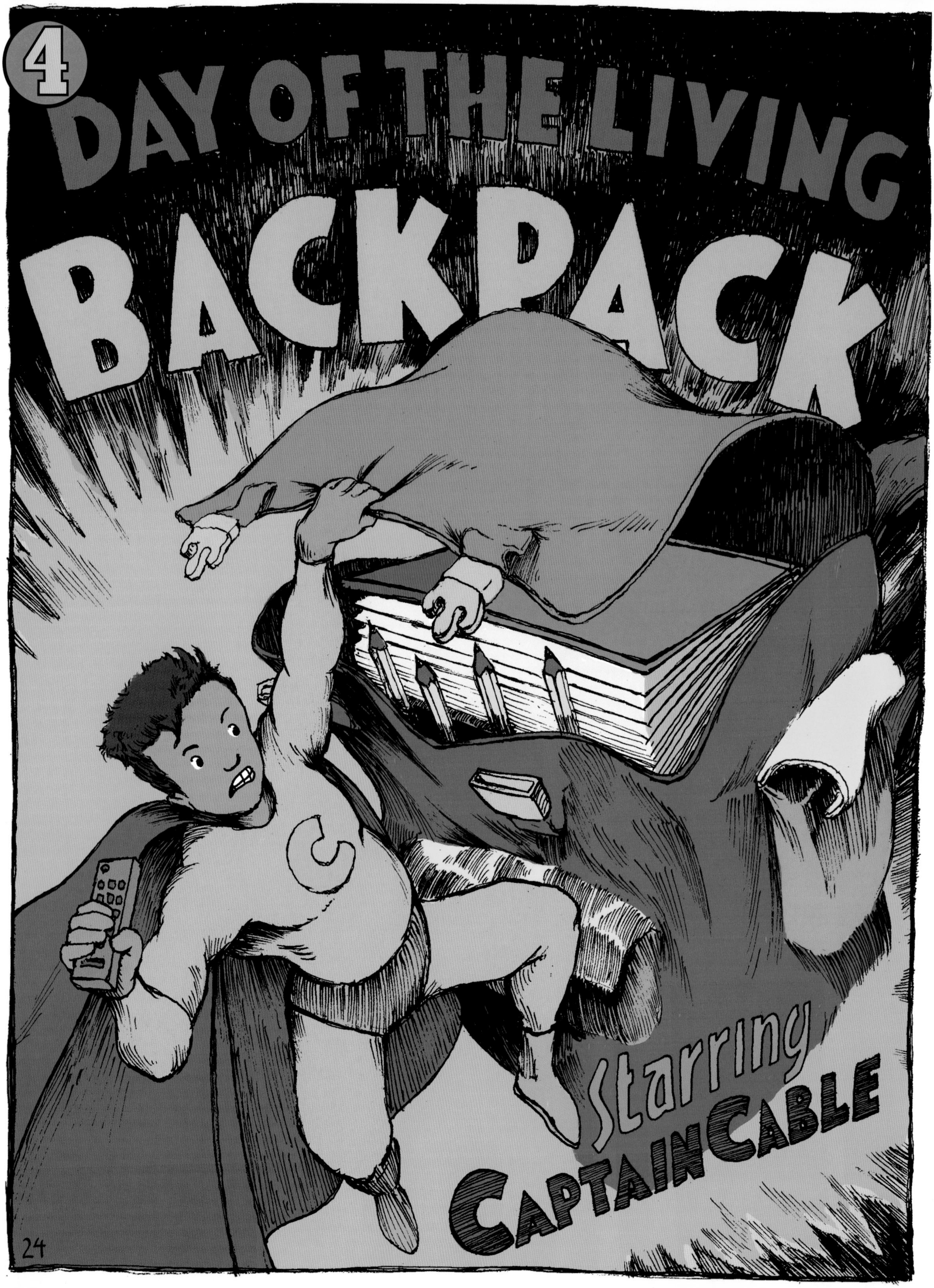
4
DAY OF THE LIVING
BACKPACK
Starring
CAPTAIN CABLE

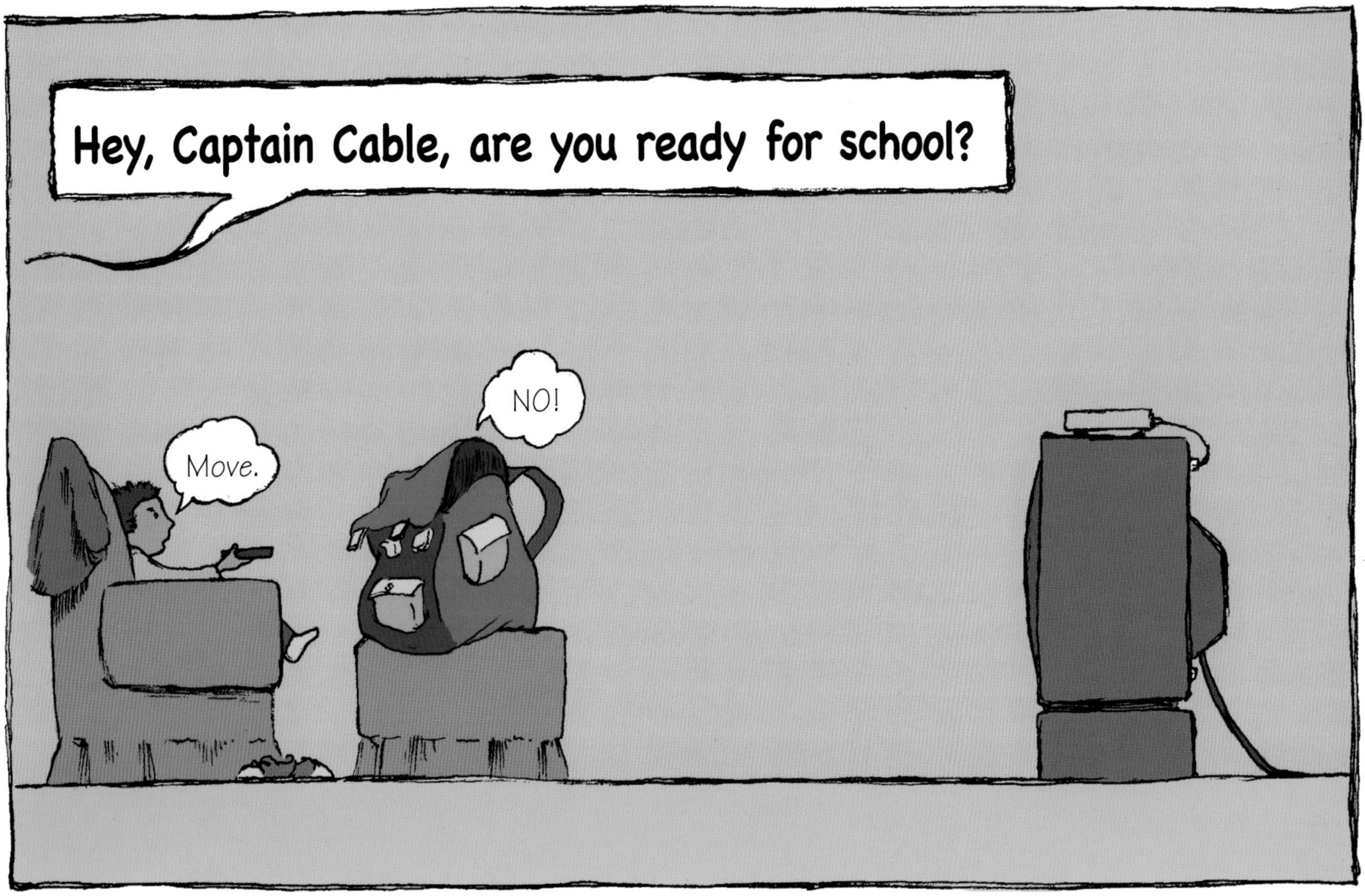
Hey, Captain Cable, are you ready for school?
Move.
NO!

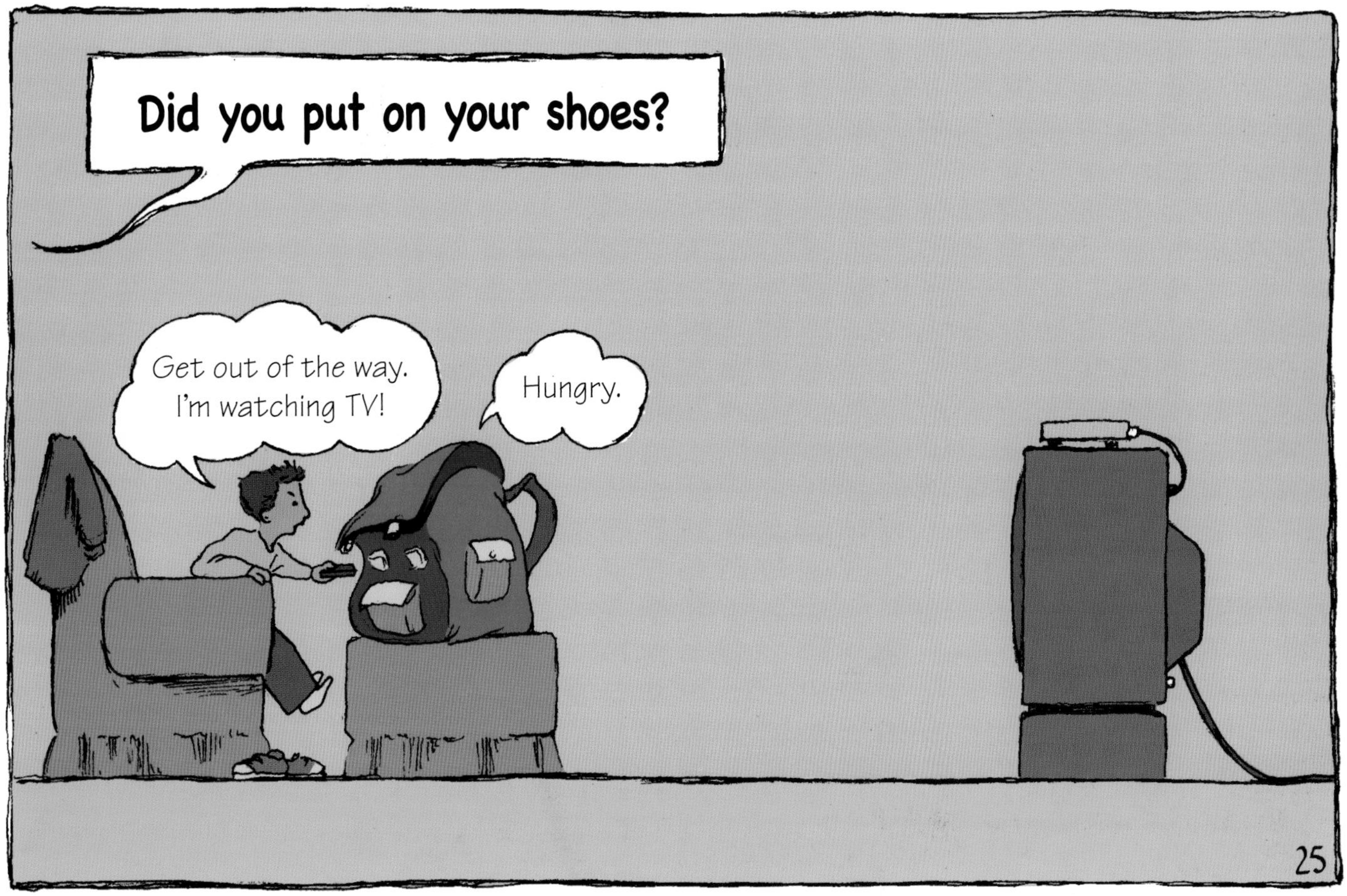
Did you put on your shoes?
Get out of the way.
I'm watching TV!
Hungry.

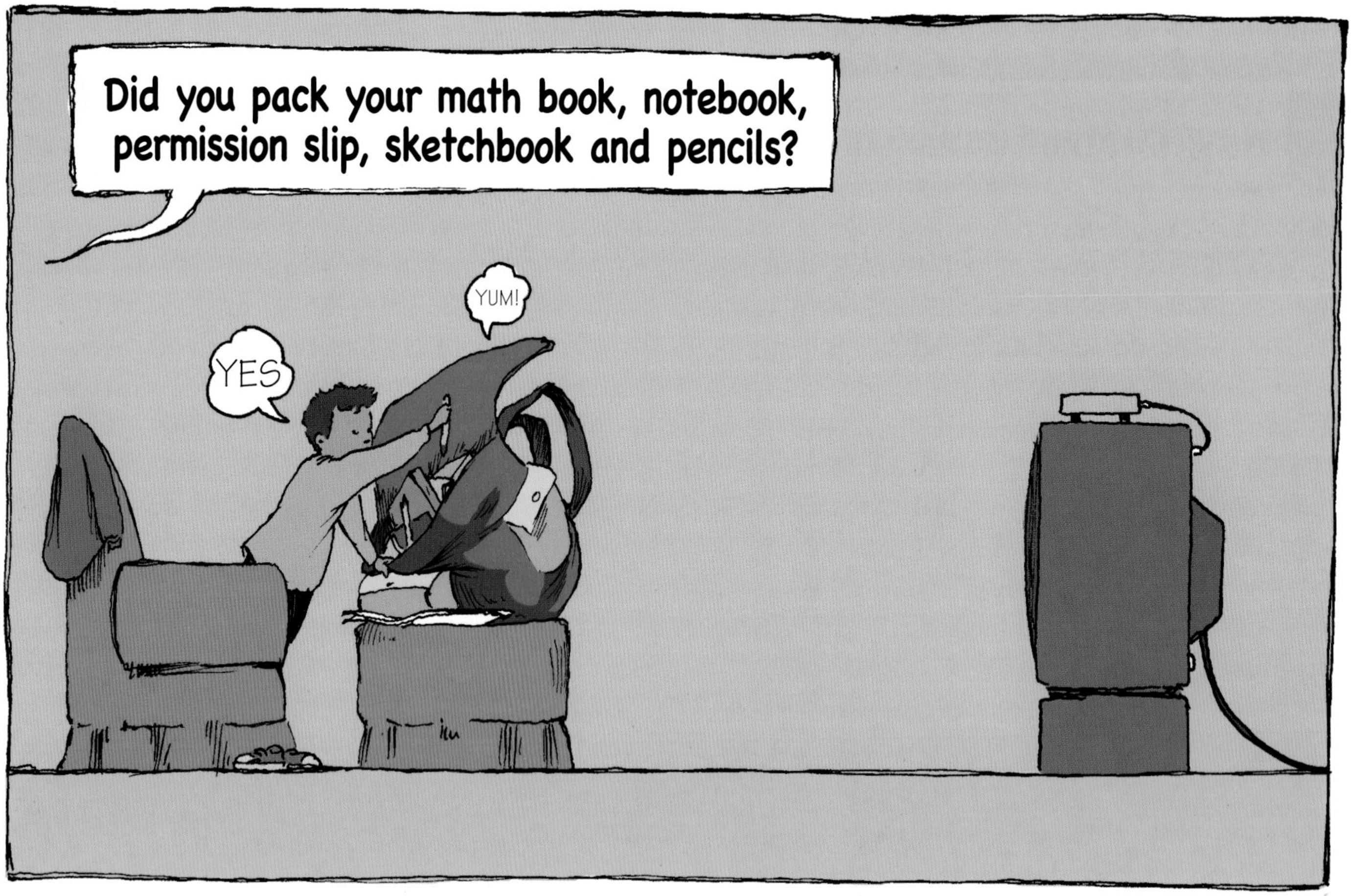
Did you pack your math book, notebook, permission slip, sketchbook and pencils?
YES
YUM!

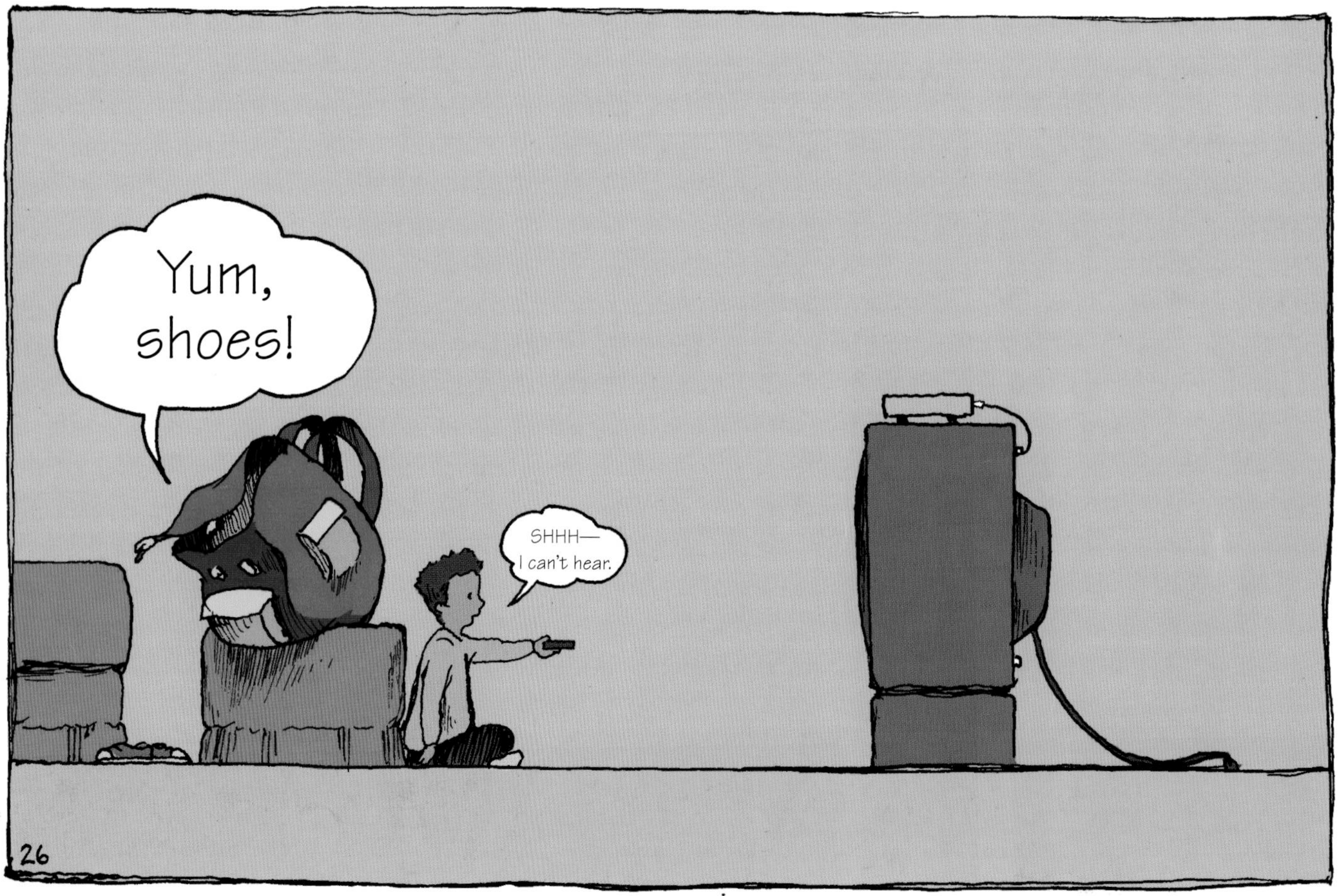
Yum, shoes!
SHHH— I can't hear.

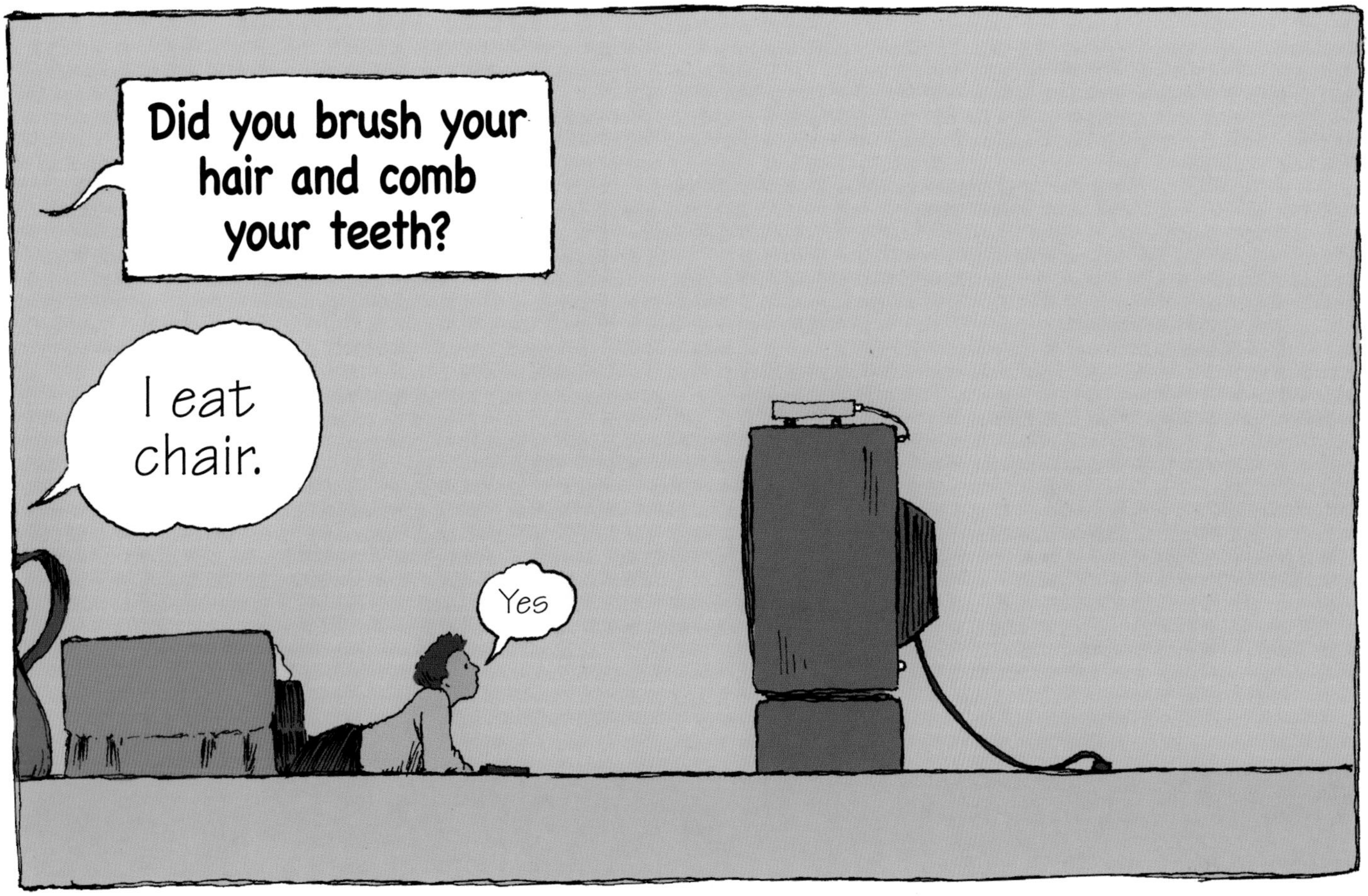
Did you brush your hair and comb your teeth?
I eat chair.
Yes

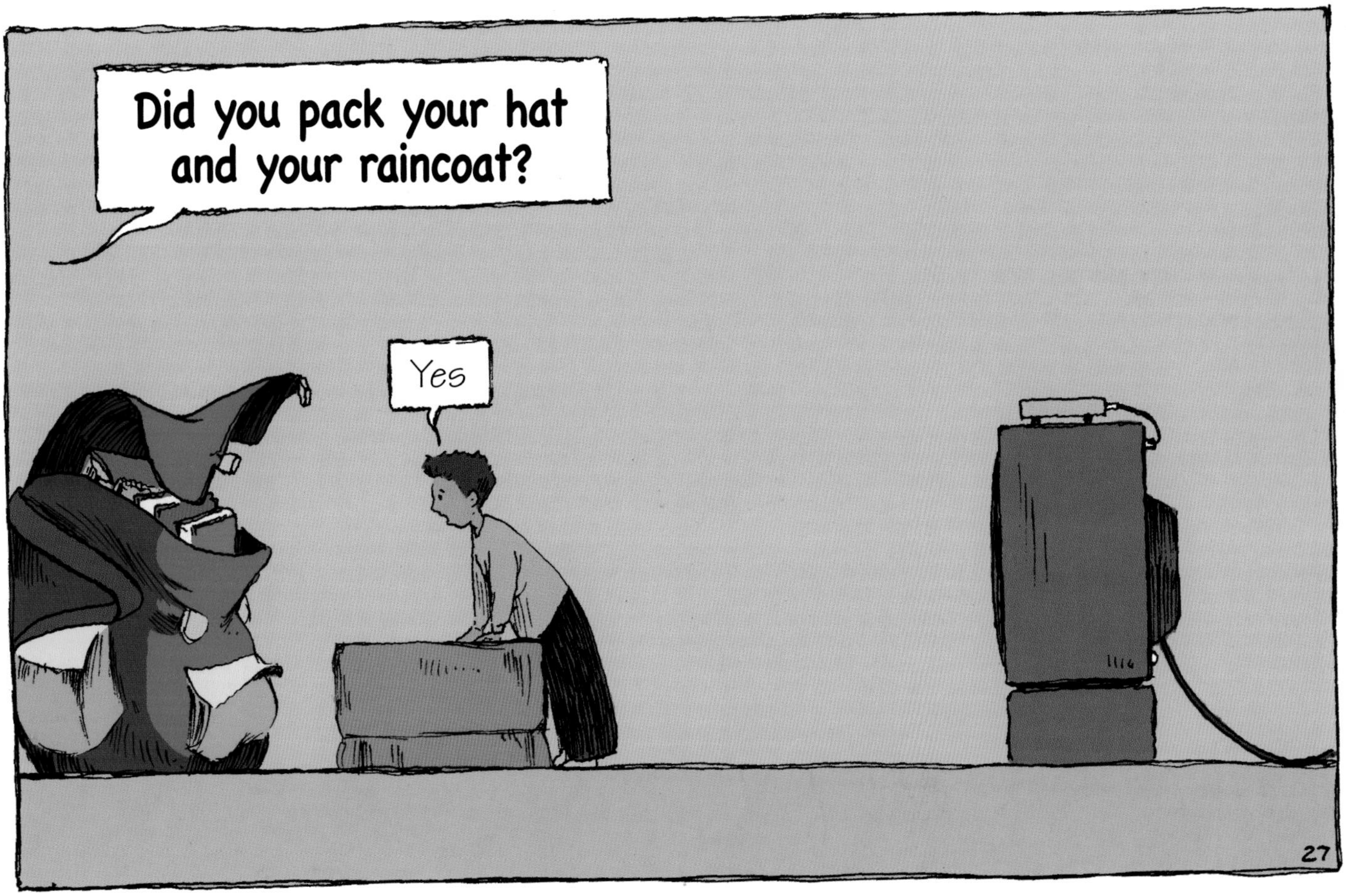
Did you pack your hat and your raincoat?
Yes

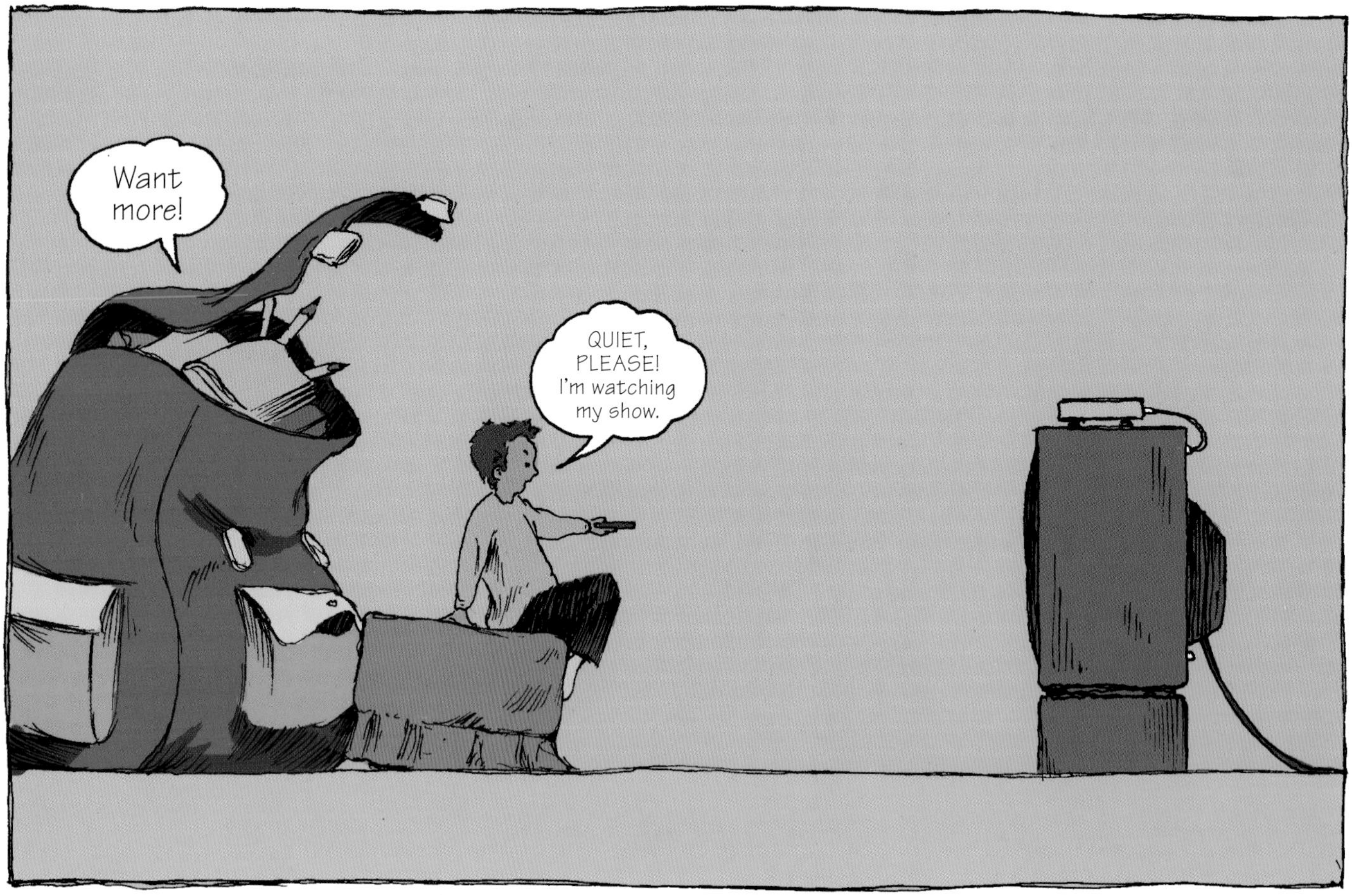
Want more!
QUIET, PLEASE! I'm watching my show.

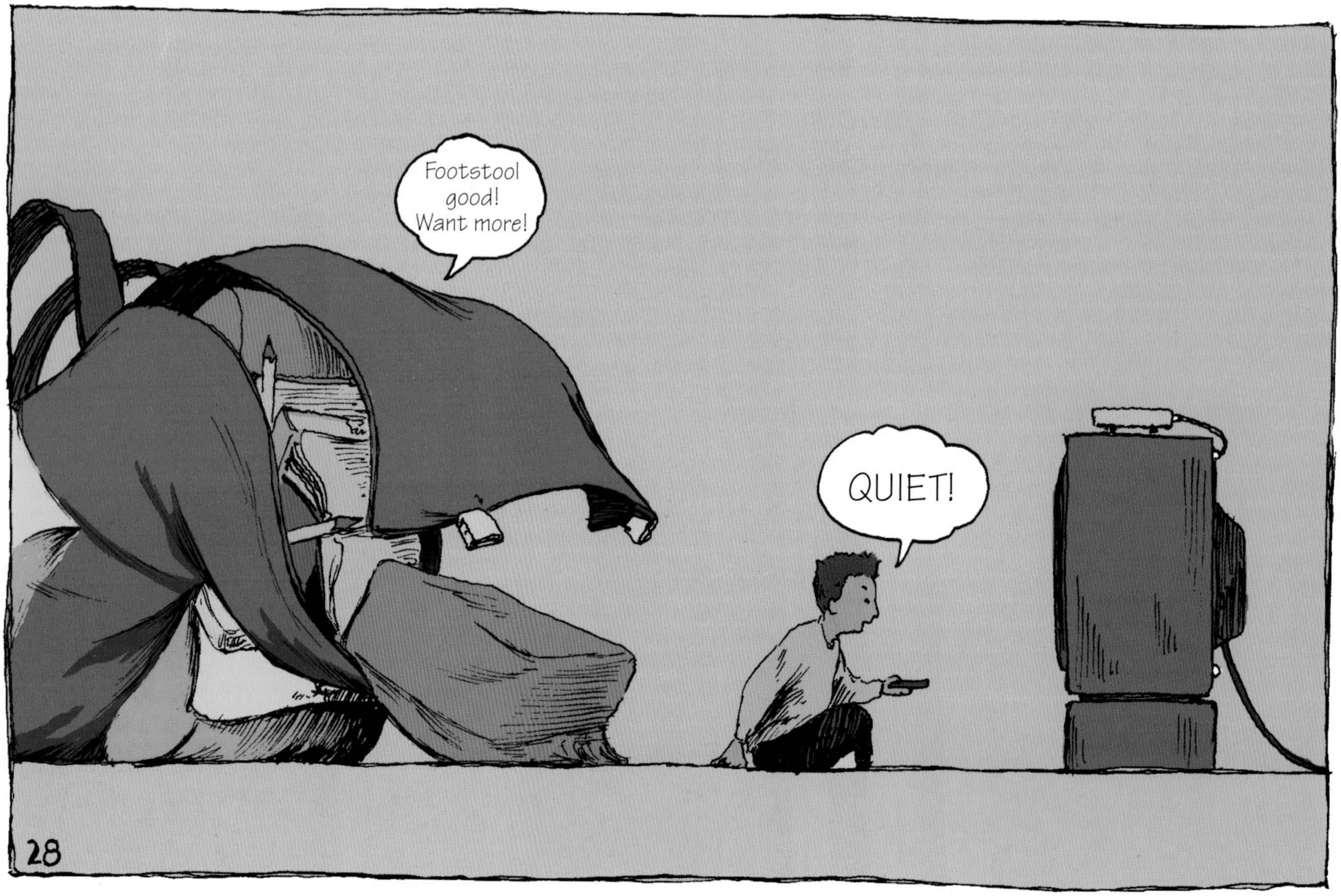
Footstool good! Want more!
QUIET!

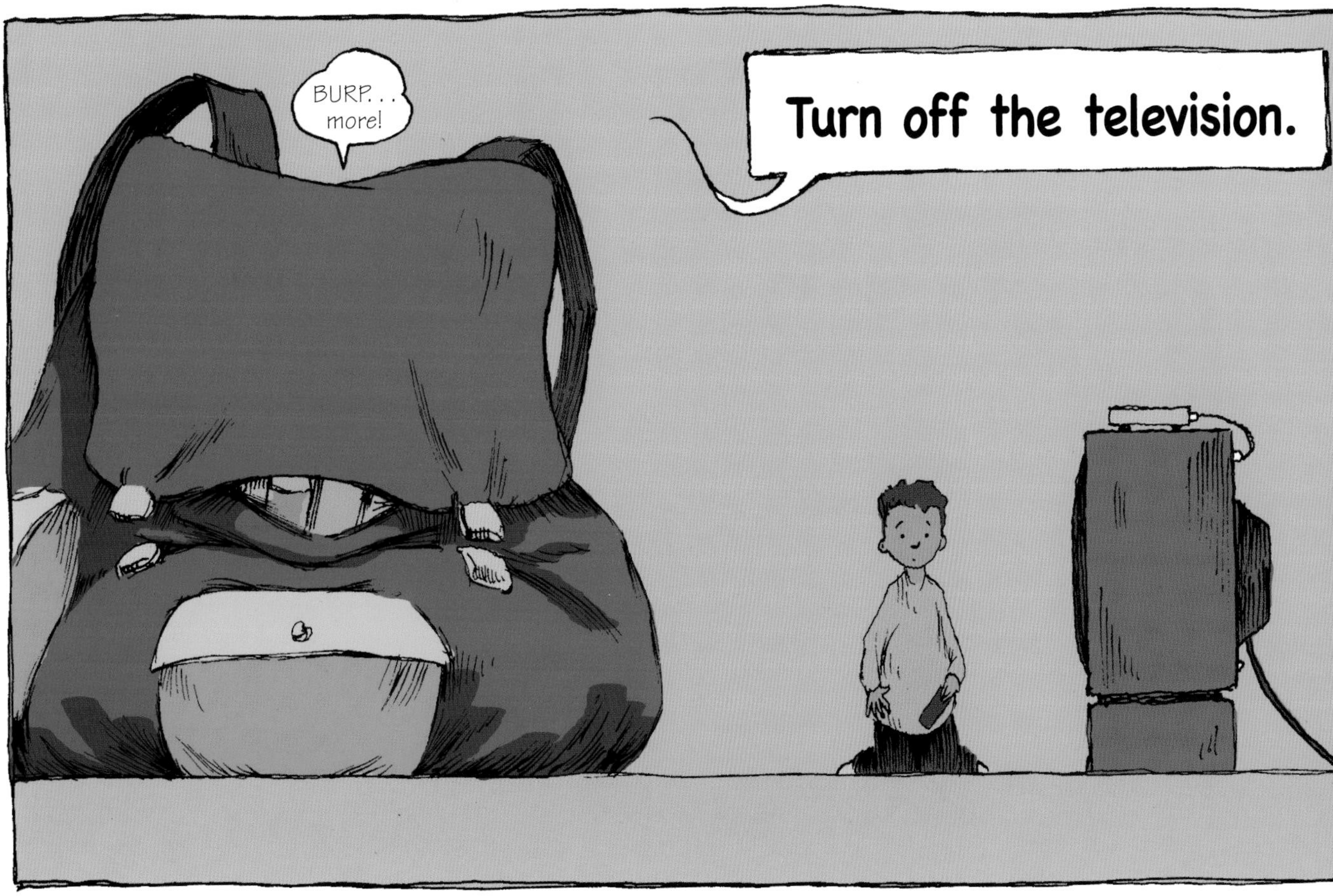
BURP. . .
more!
Turn off the television.

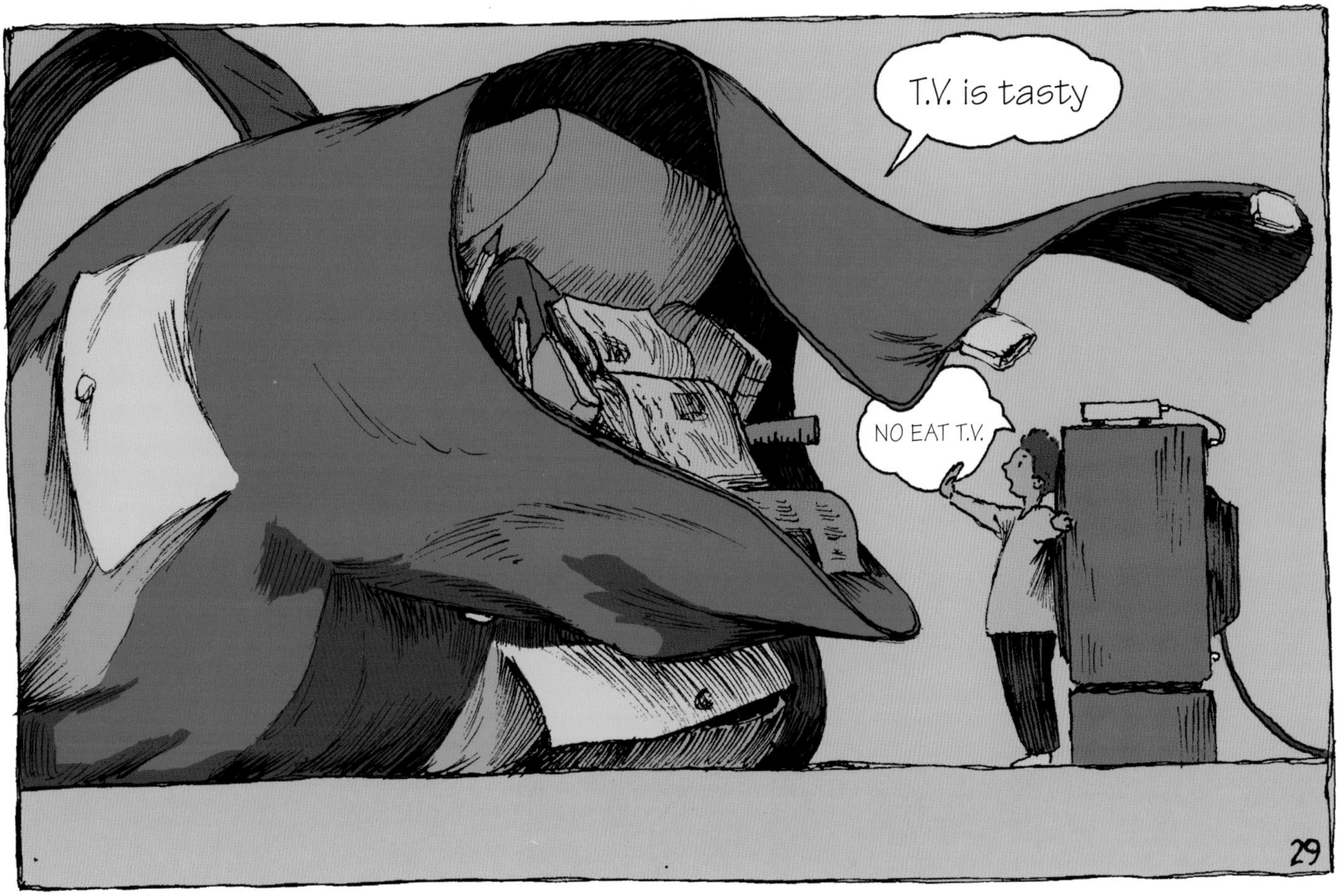
T.V. is tasty
NO EAT T.V.

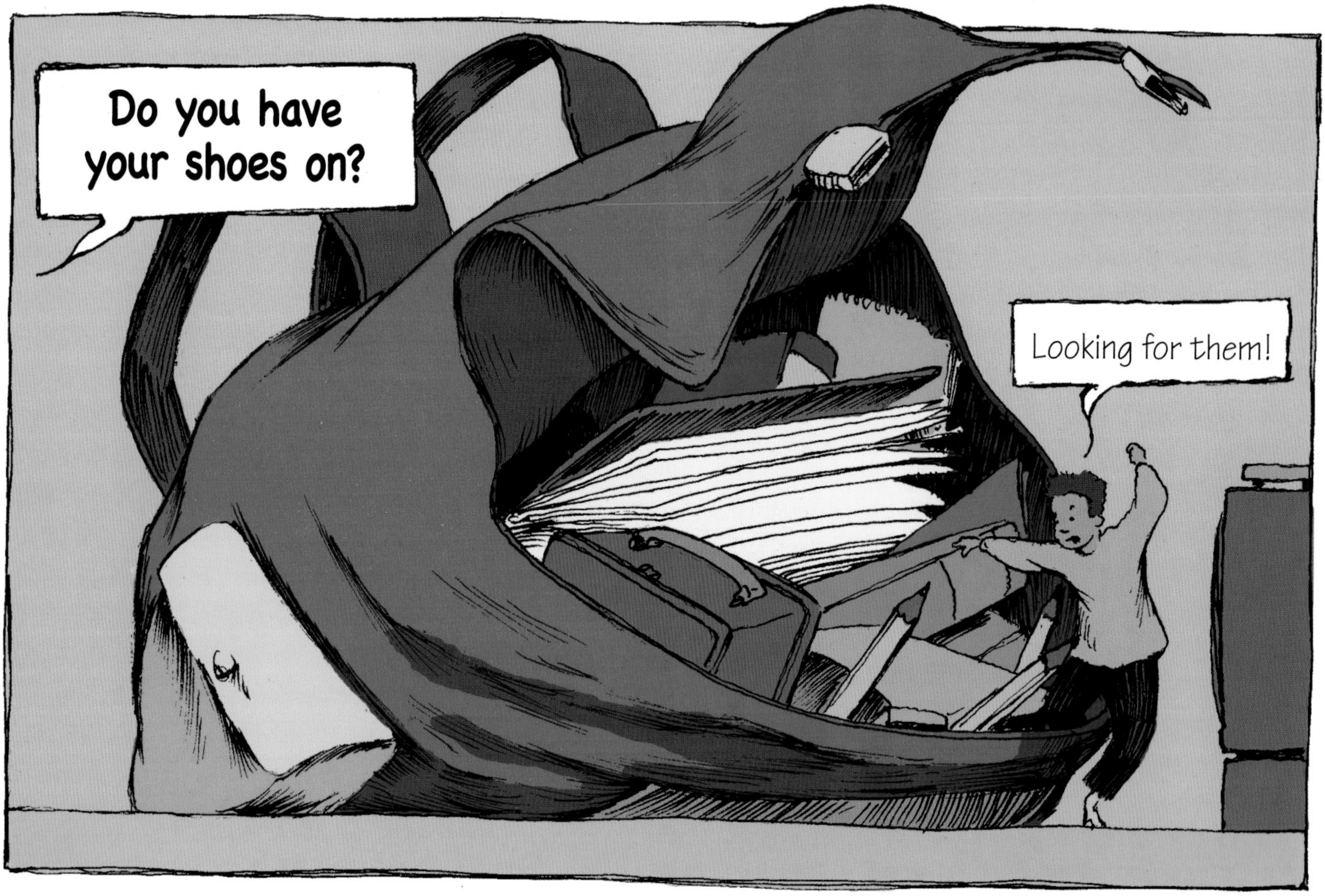
Do you have your shoes on?
Looking for them!

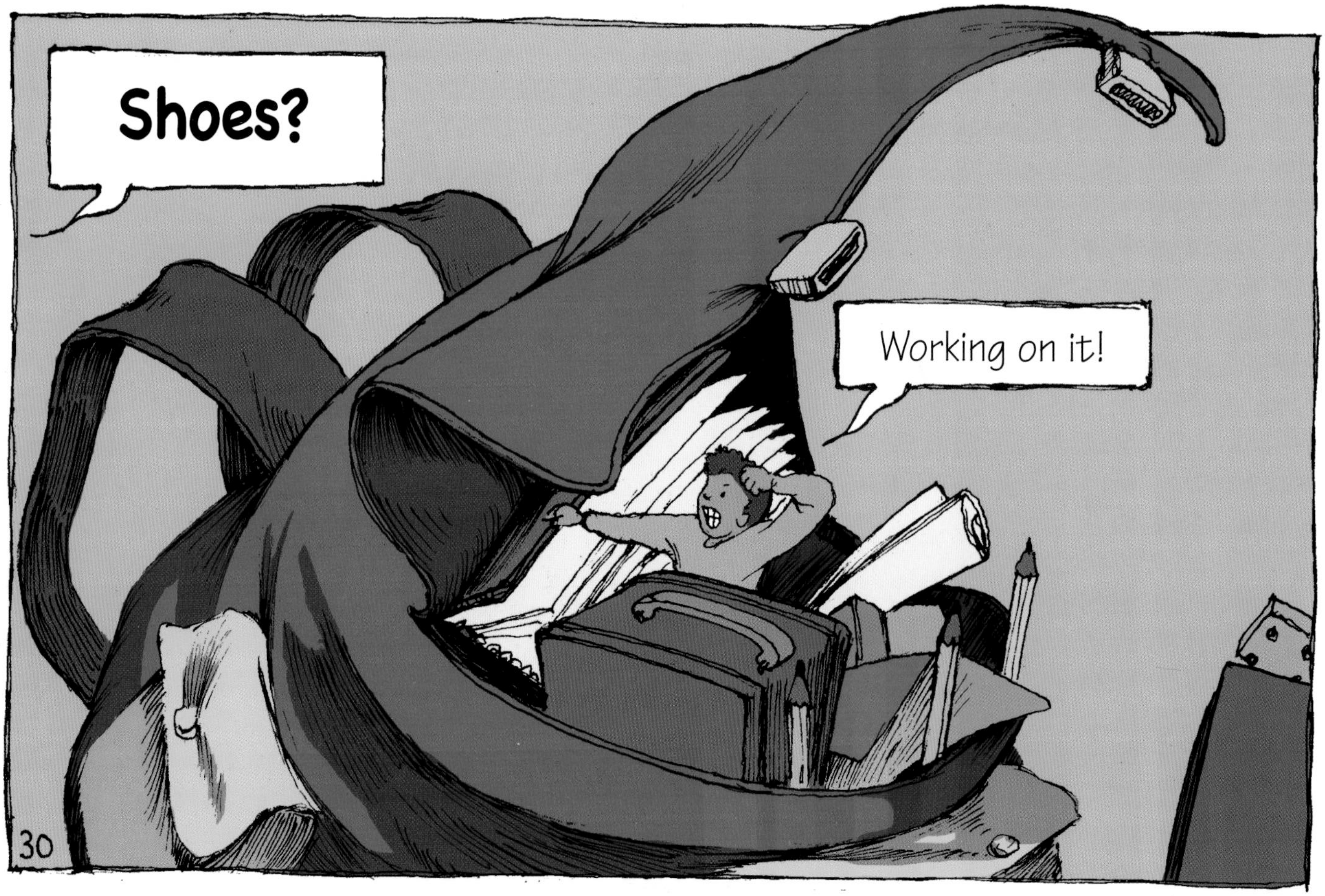
Shoes?
Working on it!